THE EYES THAT KEPT A SECRET

VOLUME 1

JUDGE MANYONGA

GONDO VISION

VOLUME 1

THE EYES THAT KEPT A SECRET

CONTENTS

PREFACE

We often say that love is blind.

But what if it isn't? What if it sees everything... and simply chooses to look away?

This story began with a lie , a beautiful, quiet lie I told not just to the world, but to the woman who once held my heart like it was sacred. A lie about what I could see... and what I couldn't. They say regaining sight is a miracle. But sometimes, seeing too much is the curse.

In the days following my recovery, I became something I never imagined: a man hiding behind vision. I watched the world pretend around me, friends, neighbors, even Grace, each moving within a carefully choreographed dance of trust and appearances. But trust is a fragile illusion. And secrets, like shadows, only grow longer in the light.

As you turn these pages, remember this: **Every truth has its price. And some eyes were never meant to see it.**

— **David**

INTRODUCTION

THE EYES THAT KEPT A SECRET

"Some secrets are like shadows – they cling to you, slipping into every corner of your life, whispering doubts when you close your eyes, and tightening their grip as the days turn into nights."

Welcome to **"The Eyes That Kept a Secret,"** a story about love, betrayal, and the haunting power of unspoken truths. At its heart, this novel is about a man who regained his sight but chose to keep it hidden, hoping to see the world as it truly was, unfiltered by pretense and pity.

David Hughes' journey from darkness to light is not just a physical transformation, but a psychological reckoning. He becomes a silent observer in his own life, watching as the threads of his marriage slowly unravel before his newly opened eyes. It's a story that explores the thin line between love and resentment, trust and betrayal, and the lengths we go to protect the ones we love – even from ourselves.

As you read through these pages, you will walk with David through the silent corridors of his doubt, feel the heavy weight of his secrets, and wrestle with the moral choices that define his path. You will see the world through his conflicted eyes, torn between revealing the truth and clinging to the comfort of old lies.

Prepare to be pulled into a world where **secrets are silent weapons**, and every glance, every whispered word, becomes a potential turning point. This is not just a story about sight – it's a story about seeing the truth, even when it hurts.

I invite you to take this journey with me, to peer into the hearts of these characters and perhaps, in the process, discover a bit of your own truth.

Happy reading.

CHAPTER 1

Miracle Surgery

David Hughes had always known darkness. It was the constant backdrop to his life, a heavy curtain that had closed around him years ago, robbing him of sight and, for a time, hope. But now, that darkness had been lifted. The miracle surgery had been a success. The bandages came off, and his world exploded into color, light, and a chaos of forgotten details. He could see – clearly, painfully, overwhelmingly – but only he knew it. And for now, he intended to keep it that way.

It started in the cold, antiseptic light of a hospital room. David remembered the sterile smell, the hum of machines, the light touch of the nurse as she gently peeled back the gauze. The blur of shapes slowly sharpened into defined edges. The doctor's face came into focus – a middle-aged man with a well-trimmed beard and a smile that cracked his professional facade.

"David, can you see me?" the doctor had asked, his voice tight with anticipation.

David had blinked, feeling the burn of light for the first time in years. He had paused, let his eyes adjust, then nodded.

"Yes," he whispered, his voice a raw rasp. "I can see you."

The room had erupted into muted cheers, the nurse squeezing his shoulder, the doctor scribbling furiously on his clipboard. But in the back of David's mind, a thousand questions raced. What would this new world look like? Would it be the same one he remembered from before, or had it changed in his absence? Had he changed?

But one question drowned out all the others – **What had Grace been doing while he was blind?**

The first day back home was surreal. The world felt too bright, the walls too close, the rooms too small. He had learned to navigate the house by touch, counting steps and feeling textures, but now he found himself stumbling over corners and bumping into door frames as if he were the blind one again.

Grace had been at work when he returned. She had left a note on the kitchen counter, written in her familiar, looping script:

"Welcome home, love. Dinner's in the fridge. Be back soon. Can't wait to see you. – G"

David stared at the note, the simple words blurring as his eyes struggled to keep up. It was the first time in years he had actually read something, and the realization hit him like a punch to the gut. For a moment, he simply stood there, gripping the edge of the counter, his heart thundering in his chest.

When Grace finally came home that evening, David was sitting in his old armchair by the window, the dim light casting long shadows across the living room. He had chosen this spot deliberately – out of the direct line of the door, where he could watch her without being immediately seen.

The door creaked open, and Grace stepped inside, her heels clicking softly against the hardwood floor. She was talking on the phone, her voice low and musical, a tone she rarely used with him anymore.

"I know... yes... I'll try to come by this weekend... no, he's still adjusting... yes, I miss you too," she whispered, pausing by the coat rack to slip off her jacket.

David's jaw tightened. He felt the old, familiar ache of suspicion creeping into his bones. It was a feeling he had tried to ignore for years, a nagging doubt that had whispered to him in the darkness. But now, with his eyes wide open, he could see the subtle cues – the way she hesitated before hanging up, the slight smile she wore as she slipped the phone into her purse.

She turned, her eyes finally landing on him. For a split second, her face froze in a strange, unreadable expression – a flash of something close to guilt – before it melted into a broad, practiced smile.

"David! You're up! How are you feeling?" she asked, crossing the room quickly to plant a kiss on his cheek. He felt the coldness of her lips, the disconnect between her words and her body language.

"Getting there," he replied, forcing a smile as his mind raced.

Later that night, as Grace prepared dinner, David pretended to struggle his way to the kitchen, fumbling slightly against the door frame for effect. He knew his steps were too confident, his movements too precise, and he forced himself to slow down, to stumble a bit, to **act** blind.

Grace glanced over her shoulder, her eyes narrowing for just a moment before she turned back to the stove.

"How was your day, love?" she asked, her tone light but strained, the clatter of the wooden spoon against the pot a bit too forceful.

David took a deep breath, steadying his nerves. He needed to be careful, to play his part perfectly.

"Same as always," he replied, reaching out to find his seat at the kitchen table. "Just... finding my way."

She chuckled, a tight, uneasy sound. "I'm sure you'll get the hang of it soon. You've always been a fast learner."

David forced a laugh, feeling the weight of his deception growing heavier. He had never thought of himself as a liar, but then again, he had never thought he would have to be.

As the days stretched into weeks, David's silent observation continued. He noticed the small things first – the way Grace spent more time on her phone, the hushed conversations she took in the other room, the faint whiff of unfamiliar cologne on her clothes.

He kept his newfound sight a secret, becoming a ghost in his own home, a silent spectator to his wife's shifting world. He watched as she slipped off her wedding ring while texting late at night, as she suddenly became more protective of her phone, as she started working longer hours without explanation.

Every day, David's vision grew sharper, both literally and figuratively. He began to see the cracks in his marriage, the lies that had slipped past him in the darkness, and the painful, unavoidable truth that he had been a blind man in more ways than one.

But he said nothing. He simply watched, waiting for the right moment to reveal his secret. **When that moment came, he intended to be ready.**

That Friday, the rain came down hard, drumming against the windows in a relentless cascade. The air felt thick, suffocating, as if the walls themselves were holding their breath. David had spent the morning listening to the weather reports, the static crackle of the radio a comforting reminder of his old world, the one without sight. But now, he was awake – painfully, intensely awake – and his eyes missed nothing.

Grace came home late that evening, her hair damp, her coat dripping small puddles onto the hardwood floor. She fumbled with her keys, her breath coming in short, nervous bursts. David, sitting in his usual armchair, turned his head slightly as if reacting to the sound, but he had been watching her through the rain-streaked window long before she crossed the threshold.

"David?" she called, her voice rising above the steady patter of rain. "I'm home."

"In the living room," he replied, trying to keep his tone steady, his eyes fixed on the shadow she cast in the hallway. He noticed the way she hesitated, her hand tightening around the strap of her handbag before she forced a smile onto her face and stepped into the room.

"You didn't call today," he said casually, his head tilted slightly in her direction. "Long day?"

Grace paused, her fingers freezing in the act of unbuttoning her coat. She looked at him, eyes searching his face for a clue, a hint that he might know more than he let on. But David's expression remained calm, his gaze seemingly unfocused, the perfect mask of a blind man.

"Yeah," she replied, her tone a bit too quick, a bit too high. "Just… a lot of meetings. You know how it is."

David nodded, forcing a small, tight-lipped smile. "I'm sure."

She slipped off her shoes, her movements stiff, and crossed the room to place her bag on the side table. She didn't notice the slight tremble in her own hands, but David did.

He let a beat pass, then added, "I heard you laughing when you came up the driveway."

Grace froze, her back to him, her shoulders tense. "Laughing?" she repeated, forcing a light chuckle. "Oh, must have been a podcast. You know I like those silly true crime ones."

David felt a cold, sharp thrill creep up his spine. He had seen her through the window, laughing, head tilted back, phone to her ear. There had been a softness in her posture, a relaxed, unguarded happiness that had vanished the moment she crossed the threshold.

"Ah, right," he said, leaning back into his chair, folding his hands in his lap. "Those can be pretty funny. Sometimes I can almost hear you smiling from the living room."

There it was. A subtle test, a light pressure on a crack in the wall. Grace's breath hitched for a fraction of a second before she forced another laugh, a brittle, strained sound.

"Yeah, they can be pretty entertaining," she said, turning quickly toward the kitchen. "I'll, uh, get us some tea. You must be tired."

David's eyes followed her retreating figure, his heart pounding with a mixture of guilt and grim satisfaction. He could feel the walls closing in, the space between them tightening with every unspoken word.

As he listened to the clink of cups and the soft rush of boiling water, David let his eyes drift over to her handbag, still perched on the side table. The phone inside it vibrated once, then fell silent.

She was lying.

David's fingers curled into fists, his mind racing. He had never wanted this, never wanted to be the suspicious, secretive husband. But the truth was there, sharp and undeniable, just like the light that now cut through his once-darkened world.

He closed his eyes, leaning his head back against the chair, and exhaled slowly. **If Grace had secrets, then so would he. For now.**

Later that evening, they sat at the dinner table, the clatter of cutlery against ceramic plates filling the silence between them. Grace had cooked – her signature lemon-garlic chicken with rosemary potatoes – a meal she often made when trying to smooth over a rough patch. David's senses, sharper than ever, caught the faint traces of perfume lingering in the air, a scent different from her usual floral notes. Something muskier, more daring. He filed the detail away, his mind a quiet, whirring machine.

Grace reached for the salt shaker, her fingers brushing the edge of her wine glass, and David instinctively reached out to steady it before it tipped over. His hand shot forward, catching the glass just as it wobbled, his grip firm and precise.

Grace froze, her eyes snapping up to his face, a small frown creasing her brow. For a moment, the only sound was the soft hum of the refrigerator in the corner, the clink of silverware forgotten.

"How... how did you know it was falling?" she asked, her voice tinged with confusion.

David's heart skipped a beat. He had moved without thinking, his instincts honed over weeks of silent observation. He forced a slow, easy smile, leaning back in his chair as if he hadn't just stumbled toward disaster.

"Sound," he replied, tapping his ear. "I heard it tip."

Grace blinked, her frown deepening, but then she seemed to dismiss the thought, giving a small, relieved laugh. "Of course. You've always had great reflexes."

David exhaled quietly, feeling the tension seep from his shoulders. She had bought it – for now. But he knew the slip had been close, too close. He couldn't afford mistakes like this, not if he was to keep his newfound sight a secret until he figured out exactly what Grace had been hiding.

They returned to their meal, but the atmosphere had shifted, the air between them charged with unspoken questions. David kept his head tilted slightly, his eyes focused just over Grace's shoulder, his mind calculating every word, every glance.

He would have to be more careful. The world was no longer

a dark, quiet void, and every movement, every gesture, every glance now carried a new, dangerous potential.

For David, the dance had begun.

CHAPTER 2

Shadows and Secrets

David had always appreciated the quiet of early mornings. Before his accident, he would wake up with the first hint of dawn, slip into his running shoes, and hit the fog-kissed streets of their quiet Melbourne suburb. It was his time to think, to plan, to visualize his goals. But now, as the sun filtered through the blinds of their master bedroom, casting thin lines of light across his face, the mornings felt more like a game of deception.

He lay still, his body tense but his breathing steady, listening to the soft, even breaths of Grace beside him. He had memorized every rise and fall of her chest, every subtle shift of the mattress, the gentle rustle of sheets as she dreamed. But today, the morning felt different – sharp, tinged with an unfamiliar tension.

Careful not to disturb her, he slowly sat up, his bare feet sinking into the thick, plush carpet. He glanced around the room, his eyes catching the morning light glinting off Grace's wedding ring, carelessly left on the dresser. It was a small thing, a detail most would miss, but for David, it felt like a signal. She had never been one to take off her ring – not even for dishwashing.

Sliding into his robe, he stepped out into the hallway, the cool air of the house brushing against his face. He padded quietly toward the kitchen, the familiar path still etched into his muscle memory from years of navigating his world without sight.

As he reached for the coffee pot, he heard the distant creak of their old front gate. His pulse quickened. He had grown more attuned to the sounds of their home in his blindness, every creak, every groan of the aging wooden beams a familiar echo in his mind. But this was different – a small, quick rustle, followed by the faint tap of footsteps on their gravel path.

Peering through the kitchen window, he caught sight of their neighbor, Fiona Turner, a woman in her late fifties with a hawk-like nose and a wardrobe full of pastel floral prints. Fiona was the unofficial eyes and ears of the neighborhood, a self-appointed watchtower who kept an iron grip on the pulse of their cul-de-sac.

She paused near their mailbox, leaning forward slightly as if listening for something, her sharp eyes scanning the windows. David quickly stepped back, heart thudding. Had she seen him? Was she trying to catch a glimpse of the supposedly blind man moving about his house with too much confidence?

He cursed under his breath, feeling the familiar tightness creep into his chest. He had to be more careful. His secret was a fragile thing, a glass house built on a foundation of lies and half-truths.

As he turned back to the counter, he heard Grace's soft footsteps approaching from the hallway. She entered the kitchen, her dark hair spilling over her shoulders, her eyes still soft with sleep.

"Morning," she murmured, leaning against the counter beside him. He felt her fingers brush his arm – a small, instinctive touch, but one that felt charged, like she was checking for something.

"Morning," he replied, forcing his tone into the careful, deliberate cadence he had perfected over the months. He could feel her eyes on him, searching his face for... what?

"Did you sleep well?" she asked, her voice light, but with an undertone he couldn't quite place.

"Well enough," he replied, pouring coffee into his favorite mug. He felt her hand linger a moment too long before she pulled back, reaching for her own cup.

For a moment, the kitchen was filled with the quiet clinking of mugs and the soft hum of the refrigerator. Then, just as he was about to retreat to his usual corner of the living room, Grace's phone buzzed on the counter between them.

David's head snapped toward the sound, his heart giving a sharp, reflexive kick. He had become hyper-aware of Grace's phone habits in recent weeks. Late-night messages. Quick, whispered phone calls from the bathroom. The way she sometimes turned her body just slightly when texting, her back to him as if protecting her secrets.

Grace glanced at the screen, her eyes flicking quickly over the message before she tilted the phone away, sliding it into her pocket with a casualness that felt too practiced.

David's jaw tightened.

"Work?" he asked, his tone deliberately light, tipping the balance between curiosity and casual indifference.

Grace hesitated for a fraction of a second, then gave a small, tight smile. "Yeah, just some early morning updates from the office."

"On a Saturday?"

She paused, her fingers tightening around her mug. "Yeah, you know how it is. Busy season."

David held his breath, letting the silence stretch between them. He knew Grace's office well – a financial advisory firm that rarely, if ever, demanded weekend work.

He forced a small, tight-lipped smile, reaching for his coffee. "Of course. Gotta keep the clients happy."

Grace nodded, her eyes flicking to the window, where Fiona's shadow had disappeared from the front yard. For a moment, David thought he saw a flicker of relief pass over her face, but then it was gone, replaced by the familiar, composed expression he had grown so used to.

As she turned to leave, her phone buzzed again – a single, sharp vibration that sent a jolt through both of them. David's fingers clenched around his mug, his knuckles turning white.

Grace didn't look back as she left the kitchen, her steps quick, her form tense.

David stared at the empty doorway, his mind racing.

Secrets had a way of building like storm clouds on the horizon, darkening the landscape before the first drop of rain even touched the ground. And as he stood alone in the kitchen, the bitter taste of coffee on his tongue, David knew that the first drops had already started to fall.

As the morning sun climbed higher, casting long, golden streaks across the polished wooden floors, David leaned against the cool marble of the kitchen counter, his mind still swirling with the brief but tense exchange with Grace. He had learned to trust his instincts, the same instincts that had kept him alive in the darkest moments of his recovery. Something was off.

The front gate creaked again, a slow, drawn-out groan that set his teeth on edge. He peered through the thin slit in the blinds, catching a glimpse of Fiona Turner, the self-appointed neighborhood watch, as she lingered by his mailbox once more. She was crouched low, her hawkish eyes trained on something hidden just out of view.

David felt a surge of irritation. Fiona had always been a busybody, the kind of woman who took it upon herself to monitor the comings and goings of the entire street, from the mailman's irregular deliveries to the stray cats that occasionally wandered into her flowerbeds. But this was different. She had never been so openly nosy before.

He watched as Fiona slowly straightened, her fingers adjusting the collar of her floral blouse, her eyes flicking nervously toward the house before she turned and marched back to her own front door, her small, precise steps kicking up tiny puffs of gravel as she went.

David exhaled slowly, his mind racing. He needed to keep a tighter grip on his secret. Fiona had sharp eyes, and the last thing he needed was for her to catch a glimpse of him moving with too much certainty, too much awareness.

His thoughts drifted back to the moment he had first realized his sight was returning. It had been a month after the surgery – a cold, rainy morning. Grace had left for work, the soft click of her heels on the hardwood floor echoing through their silent home. David had been sitting in his favorite armchair by the window, his mind a chaotic blend of hope and despair, when he noticed it. A thin, blurry sliver of light. Just a whisper of brightness at the edge of his vision.

At first, he had thought it was a trick of his mind, a cruel hallucination born from months of darkness and desperation. But as he focused, the light grew stronger, like the first rays of dawn breaking through a storm. He had reached out, trembling, his fingers brushing against the fabric of the curtain, the rough weave sharp and real beneath his fingertips.

He had wanted to scream, to shout for joy, but fear had clamped down on his throat like a vice. What if it was temporary? What if it faded as quickly as it had come, leaving him more broken than before?

Instead, he had sat there, his heart pounding like a war drum, as the sliver of light expanded into shapes, shadows, and the faint, ghostly outlines of the world he had once taken for granted.

From that day forward, he had kept his secret, nurturing it like a fragile ember, terrified that the slightest breath of wind would snuff it out.

David forced himself to shake off the memory, his grip tightening around the cool handle of his coffee mug. He couldn't afford to let his mind wander. Not now. Not when the walls were closing in.

He made his way to the living room, carefully navigating the familiar contours of their furniture. He settled into his armchair, his eyes drifting to the window, where Fiona's curtains had fluttered shut like a stage closing on a suspenseful act.

Moments later, Grace returned, her phone still clutched tightly in her hand, her eyes distant, unfocused. She paused at the doorway, her gaze lingering on him for a moment longer than usual, as if trying to read something in his expression.

"You okay?" she asked, her tone light but her eyes sharp.

David forced a smile. "Yeah, just... thinking."

Grace hesitated, then moved to the kitchen, the soft clatter of dishes filling the silence.

David exhaled, his mind churning with the weight of his secret, the growing tension in their home, and the ever-watchful eyes of their nosy neighbor.

He had to be careful. One wrong move, one misplaced glance, and the fragile web of lies he had spun around himself would come crashing down.

That evening, as the sun dipped behind the row of Victorian terraces, casting long, finger-like shadows across the quiet street, Grace received a message that set her heart racing. It was from Mark Anderson, an old college friend she hadn't spoken to in years.

Mark: *Hey Grace! I'm in town for a conference. Would love to catch up. Drinks this weekend?*

Grace smiled, a warmth spreading through her chest as she typed a quick response. Mark had always been a good friend, the kind who never judged and always knew how to make her laugh, even during the darkest days of David's recovery.

She had just hit send when she noticed David standing in the doorway, his head tilted slightly, as if listening for the faint vibrations of her typing. She quickly locked the screen, her heart thumping a little harder than usual.

"Everything okay?" David asked, his tone casual, but his face a careful mask.

Grace forced a bright smile, sliding her phone into her back pocket. "Yeah, just a message from an old friend. Nothing major."

David hesitated, his lips parting as if to say something more, but then he simply nodded, his sightless eyes drifting to the faint sound of the evening news crackling from the living room TV.

The next morning, as David pretended to feel his way down the hallway, he caught snippets of Grace's phone conversation with Mark. Her voice was light, the kind of tone she used when she was truly happy.

"...It's been ages! I'd love to catch up. Let's do Saturday. I'll text you the details."

David clenched his jaw, a flicker of unease twisting in his gut. He had no right to feel this way – Grace had stood by him through the worst of it, through the endless doctor's appointments and sleepless nights. She deserved a break, a chance to reconnect with her old life.

But the thought of her laughing over drinks with a man from her past – a man who probably still remembered the vibrant, carefree woman she had been before his accident – made his pulse quicken with a strange, unfamiliar jealousy.

Later that day, as Grace left for work, David settled back into his armchair by the window, the morning light warm on his face. He needed to focus, to calm the growing storm in his mind. But before he could lose himself in the soothing rhythm of his breathing, he heard it – the slow, deliberate crunch of gravel underfoot.

Fiona.

David turned his head ever so slightly, just enough to catch a glimpse of her through the thin gap in the curtains. She was lingering by his mailbox again, her sharp eyes darting toward his house before she crouched low, her hands fumbling with something in the grass.

David's pulse quickened. Was she spying on him? Had she noticed something?

He forced himself to relax, his fingers curling tightly around the armrest. Fiona's nosiness was annoying, but it was also dangerous. If she suspected anything, she could blow his secret wide open.

The front gate creaked open, and David tensed as Fiona stepped onto his porch, her thin frame casting a long shadow through the frosted glass of the front door. She hesitated, her head cocked to the side as if listening for movement.

David held his breath, his mind racing. If she knocked, he would have to play his part perfectly – the cautious, sightless man who had grown used to the comforting darkness of his world.

But after a long, agonizing moment, Fiona turned and hurried back to her own house, her floral blouse fluttering in the breeze like a flag of retreat.

David exhaled slowly, his heart thundering in his chest. This was getting too close. Too risky. He needed to be more careful, to play his part more convincingly if he wanted to keep his secret safe.

As the week drew on, Grace continued to exchange messages with Mark, her mood noticeably lighter, her laughter ringing out more often as she moved around the house. David tried to ignore it, to focus on his own recovery, but he could feel the distance growing between them, a silent chasm that threatened to swallow them both.

And then, on Friday morning, as he reached for his coffee cup, David heard a sound that made his blood run cold – the soft, unmistakable click of Fiona's front door, followed by the rapid, purposeful crunch of her footsteps heading straight for his house.

He straightened, his senses on high alert as the footsteps grew louder, closer, until they paused just outside his window.

David's heart raced. If Fiona had seen him – really seen him – this could all come crashing down.

The doorbell rang just as Grace was finishing up a call with Mark, setting a lunch date for Saturday. She frowned, glancing at the wall clock. It was just past 10 a.m. – too early for any of her friends to drop by unannounced. She wiped her hands on a dish towel and headed for the door.

Standing on the other side was Fiona, her sharp eyes peering over the tops of her oversized, jewel-studded glasses. She held a plate covered in cling wrap, a smile that didn't quite reach her eyes stretching across her thin lips.

"Morning, Grace! I thought I'd drop off a little something. I made too much banana bread, and I thought you might like some."

Grace forced a smile, stepping aside to let Fiona in. "Oh, that's so kind of you, Fiona. Come on in."

As Fiona stepped into the hallway, her eyes swept over the neatly arranged shoes by the door, the soft, ambient music playing in the background, and the faint scent of freshly brewed coffee wafting from the kitchen.

"Oh, I see you're still keeping things nice and tidy. I always say a tidy house is a happy house," Fiona said, her tone dripping with passive observation.

Grace smiled tightly, leading Fiona into the kitchen. "Yes, I try my best. Coffee?"

"Oh, no, no. I can't stay long. Just wanted to drop this off and have a quick chat," Fiona said, her eyes flicking to the hallway where David's walking cane rested against the wall.

Grace noticed the direction of her gaze and felt a flicker of unease. She knew Fiona's curiosity often crossed the line into outright nosiness, but she tried to brush it off.

"David must be resting," Fiona said, her voice lowering a notch, as if trying to sound conspiratorial.

Grace forced a smile. "Yes, he's resting. The past few days have been a bit tiring for him."

Fiona leaned in a little closer, her eyes narrowing. "You know, I've been meaning to ask... I saw him the other day, out in the garden. He seemed to be moving around quite confidently. It's just... well, you know, it's surprising how well he's adapted."

Grace's heart skipped a beat. She opened her mouth to respond, but Fiona kept going.

"And just the other morning, I thought I saw him looking right at a bird that flew past your window. I thought, my goodness, he's got incredible hearing to pick up something like that." She chuckled, but her eyes remained sharp, studying Grace's face for a reaction.

Grace felt a tightness in her chest, but forced herself to laugh. "Oh, Fiona, you know David – he's got a way of making the best of a bad situation. He's always been... intuitive."

Fiona's smile tightened, her eyes never leaving Grace's face. "Yes, I suppose so. Anyway, I should be going. I'll let you get back to your day."

As Fiona made her way back down the hallway, her footsteps soft against the polished wooden floor, Grace felt a rush of relief, mixed with a twinge of doubt.

Had Fiona noticed something? Or was this just another one of her nosy neighbor routines, fishing for gossip to share over her afternoon tea?

Grace closed the door behind Fiona and leaned against it, her mind racing. She couldn't shake the feeling that Fiona's visit had been more than just a friendly gesture.

Later that evening, as Grace was busy preparing dinner, David felt the familiar vibration of her footsteps moving around the kitchen. He kept his eyes closed, his head tilted slightly, listening for the telltale sounds of stress – the sharp clatter of pans, the quick, shallow breaths.

Something had changed. He could feel it, like a storm gathering on the horizon. Grace had been quieter, more distracted, ever since Fiona's visit.

He felt a flicker of irritation. He hadn't planned on this – the meddling neighbor, the old friend rekindling old connections. His secret had been safe for months, but now, cracks were starting to form.

David clenched his fists, the old, familiar surge of anger rising in his chest. He had to be more careful. He couldn't afford a slip-up, not now, not when he was so close to… what exactly?

Freedom? Revenge? Redemption?

He didn't know anymore.

Saturday afternoon arrived, and with it, Mark. He stepped out of his rental car, stretching his tall, muscular frame as he glanced up at the house. It looked just as he remembered – neat, charming, the kind of place where memories were made and secrets were buried.

Grace met him at the door, her face lighting up as she pulled him into a warm hug. "Mark! It's so good to see you!"

David, listening from the living room, felt a cold knot form in his stomach. He recognized that tone – the soft, eager lilt in her voice, the one she used when she was genuinely happy.

He forced himself to stay calm, his fingers gripping the armrest of his chair as he listened to their muffled laughter drifting from the hallway.

Mark's deep, confident voice carried through the house. "It's been too long, Grace. I've missed this. I've missed… you."

David's jaw tightened, his heart pounding in his chest.

This was a threat.

And threats had to be dealt with.

CHAPTER 3

Whispered Suspicions

The morning sun filtered through the lace curtains of the living room, casting delicate shadows on the polished wooden floors. Grace sat at the kitchen table, her fingers wrapped around a steaming cup of tea, her mind still swirling with the warmth of yesterday's reunion with Mark. His presence had rekindled something within her, a flicker of the carefree girl she used to be. But alongside that warmth was a nagging sense of unease, like a dark cloud on the edge of a clear horizon.

She couldn't quite shake Fiona's words from a few days earlier, the offhand comment about David's remarkable awareness, the pointed way she had looked at the cane by the door. Was Fiona just being her usual nosy self, or was there something more behind those beady eyes and oversized glasses?

Grace took a deep breath, trying to push the thoughts aside. She had enough to worry about without letting her neighbor's gossip ruin her mood. She placed her cup down and moved to the sink, gazing out at the small garden where David had once spent countless hours tending to his beloved roses before the accident. Now the garden felt like a symbol of their life together, beautiful but slowly overgrown, in need of care and attention.

Two doors down, Fiona sat in her conservatory, the morning light catching the dust motes as they drifted lazily through the air. She adjusted her glasses, flipping through the morning paper without really reading it, her mind still stuck on her brief visit to Grace's house.

Something was off. She could feel it in her bones, the way a seasoned gossip senses a scandal brewing beneath the surface.

David had always been a strong, confident man, but the accident had changed everything, or so she had thought.

Her mind replayed the image of David standing in the garden, his head turning slightly as the bird fluttered past. She could swear his eyes had tracked its movement, just for a split second, before his face returned to that blank, distant stare he had adopted since losing his sight.

Fiona leaned back in her chair, a slow, predatory smile spreading across her face. If there was one thing she loved more than her prized begonias, it was uncovering the hidden dramas of her neighbors.

In the living room, David sat in his usual armchair, his face turned toward the window. He could hear the faint rustle of Grace moving around the kitchen, the clink of dishes, the soft hum of the refrigerator. It was a comforting, familiar soundscape, one that had become his world since the accident.

But beneath the calm exterior, his mind was a storm. Mark's visit had rattled him more than he cared to admit. He had felt Grace's warmth, the way her voice softened when she spoke to Mark, the easy laughter that had filled the house.

David tightened his grip on the armrest, his jaw clenching. He had to be careful. He couldn't afford another slip-up, another moment of letting his instincts take over. If Grace even suspected for a second that his blindness was a lie, everything he had worked for would crumble around him.

He forced himself to relax, taking a deep breath as he heard Grace's footsteps approaching. She entered the living room, her steps light, hesitant.

"David," she said softly, her voice carrying a note of uncertainty. "I was thinking... maybe we should have Fiona over for dinner one of these days. She's been... well, she's been a bit lonely lately, and it might be nice to catch up."

David's mind raced. Dinner with Fiona? The thought made his skin crawl. The woman was a meddler, a nosy busybody who would be watching his every move, looking for any crack in his facade. But he couldn't say no without arousing Grace's suspicions.

"That sounds... nice," he replied, forcing a smile. "It's been a while since we had a proper dinner with a friend."

Grace's face brightened, a small, relieved smile breaking through her earlier tension. "I'll give her a call later, then. It'll be good for all of us."

David nodded, but inside, he was already calculating his every move, rehearsing how to sit, how to eat, how to react without betraying his secret.

That evening, as Grace prepared to call Fiona and extend the dinner invitation, there was a sharp knock at the door. She frowned, wiping her hands on a dish towel as she moved to answer it.

Opening the door, she found Mark standing on the porch, his face serious, his dark eyes locked onto hers.

"Mark?" she said, surprised. "I wasn't expecting you."

He stepped inside without waiting for an invitation, his broad shoulders filling the hallway.

"I'm sorry for just dropping by," he said, his voice low, urgent. "But I needed to talk to you. It's about David."

Grace's heart skipped a beat, her mind flashing back to Fiona's strange, probing comments.

"What is it?" she asked, closing the door behind him.

Mark glanced around, his jaw tight. "I don't know how to say this without sounding crazy, but... something isn't right. I've been watching him, and... I don't think David is as blind as he pretends to be."

Grace felt the blood drain from her face, her knees suddenly weak. She gripped the back of a chair for support, her mind spinning.

"What... what are you talking about?" she stammered, her heart thundering in her chest.

Mark took a step closer, his eyes dark and intense. "I don't have proof. Not yet. But I've seen things, little things. The way he moves around, the way he reacts to sounds, even the way he looked at me the other day when I was leaving. Grace, I think

David has been lying to you this whole time."

Grace felt the room tilt, her world swaying beneath her feet as Mark's words sank in. She stumbled back, her grip tightening on the chair, her breath coming in short, panicked gasps.

"Mark... you can't be serious," she whispered, her eyes darting toward the living room where David sat, his head turned slightly as if listening. "That's impossible. He... he's blind. The doctors said... they said it was permanent."

Mark took a step closer, his eyes never leaving hers. "I know how it sounds, but I've seen the way he moves. The way his head turns at the slightest movement, the way he reaches for things without hesitation. I've been watching him, Grace. I can't explain it, but I know what I saw."

Grace felt her stomach twist. She had always prided herself on being a good judge of character, on knowing her husband inside and out. The idea that David could have been lying to her, that he might have been living a double life under her own roof, felt like a slap to the face.

"I... I have to sit down," she muttered, stumbling back into the kitchen and dropping into a chair. Mark followed, his broad frame seeming to fill the small space.

"Grace, I'm telling you this because I care about you. You deserve the truth," he said, his voice a rough whisper. "You need to confront him. You need to find out if he's been lying to you all this time."

Grace felt the room closing in around her, the walls pressing in like a vice. She thought back to all the little moments, the fleeting glances, the times she had caught David turning his head just a fraction too quickly, the way he had seemed to tense up when she mentioned their old vacation photos.

"Why would he do that?" she whispered, her voice breaking. "Why would he lie to me about something so... so huge?"

Mark reached out, his hand brushing her arm, his touch warm and reassuring. "I don't know. But you need to find out, Grace. For your own peace of mind."

That night, as the house settled into its usual quiet, Grace paced the living room, her bare feet brushing against the cool wooden floor. She had sent Mark away with a promise to "think about it," but her mind was already spinning with plans, with questions, with doubts.

David sat in his armchair, his face turned toward the window, his hands resting lightly on the armrests. He looked peaceful, almost serene, but Grace's eyes saw him differently now. Every breath he took, every slight movement of his head felt like a piece of a puzzle she hadn't realized she'd been piecing together for months.

"David," she said, her voice sharper than she intended.

He turned his head slightly, his face a careful mask of calm. "Yes, love?"

Grace took a deep breath, her fists clenching at her sides. "Are you... are you hiding something from me?"

David's head tilted slightly, a tiny, almost imperceptible pause before he spoke. "Hiding something? What do you mean?"

Grace stepped closer, her heart pounding so loudly she was sure he could hear it. "I don't know. Maybe the fact that you can see."

The words hung in the air like a gunshot, sharp and deafening. For a moment, the only sound in the room was the ticking of the old clock on the mantel.

David's face remained calm, his head still turned in her direction, but she saw it – the slight twitch of his jaw, the tightening of his fingers against the leather armrest.

"Grace," he said slowly, his voice measured, careful. "That's... that's a cruel thing to say."

"Is it?" she shot back, her voice rising. "Because Mark seems to think otherwise. And so does Fiona, for that matter. And now that I think about it, there have been signs, David. Little things that don't add up."

David's face remained impassive, but his hands gripped the armrests tighter, the knuckles turning white. "Mark doesn't know what he's talking about," he said, his voice a low growl. "And Fiona is a meddling old woman with too much time on her hands."

Grace took another step forward, her eyes burning with a mix of anger and hurt. "Then prove it, David. Stand up right now, walk to me without using your cane, and tell me you're blind."

David's head snapped toward her, his jaw tightening, his face a mask of barely controlled rage. For a moment, Grace thought he might actually do it, that he might stand up and walk to her, shattering the fragile illusion he had so carefully constructed.

But instead, he sank back into the chair, his hands relaxing, his face smoothing into a blank, unreadable mask.

"Grace," he said, his voice suddenly calm, almost gentle. "I know you're upset. I know this has been hard on you. But accusing me of faking my blindness... that's not fair. I'm your husband. I need you to trust me."

The words cut through her like a knife, sharp and cold. She felt the ground shift beneath her feet, the fragile foundations of her marriage cracking under the weight of her doubts.

Without another word, she turned on her heel and stormed out of the room, the sound of her footsteps echoing down the hallway.

CHAPTER 4

The First Crack

Grace didn't sleep that night. She lay awake, her mind racing, the shadows of doubt creeping into every corner of her thoughts. David's calm, measured response had felt too perfect, too controlled. She knew him well enough to sense when he was hiding something, and this time, the feeling was stronger than ever.

The next morning, she dragged herself out of bed, her eyes heavy, her thoughts muddled. She stumbled into the kitchen, flicking on the kettle as she rubbed her temples. She needed caffeine, and she needed clarity.

As she reached for the coffee tin, her gaze landed on the window. It was a small, unassuming thing, the morning light filtering through the thin, cream-colored curtains. She paused, her hand hovering over the kettle.

A memory flickered in her mind, a seemingly unimportant moment from a few weeks ago. She had been in the kitchen, cleaning up after breakfast, when David had walked past the window on his way to the garden. She had called out to him, asking if he had seen her keys, and he had turned his head slightly, his face tilted toward the window.

"By the door," he had said, his voice casual. "Near the umbrella stand."

At the time, she had brushed it off, too busy with her morning routine to question it. But now, the memory felt like a splinter in her mind, a tiny, sharp fragment that refused to be ignored.

How had he known where the keys were?

Grace's heart raced as she clutched the edge of the counter, her mind spinning. She forced herself to calm down, to think clearly. She needed more than just a vague memory. She needed proof.

Later that morning, as David sat in his usual armchair, his head tilted slightly toward the open window, Grace moved through the house with newfound purpose. She straightened the cushions, dusted the shelves, her eyes constantly flicking toward him, watching for signs, for cracks in his carefully constructed facade.

As she reached for the photo album on the coffee table, her hand paused. It was a thick, leather-bound book, the kind that creaked when you opened it, the pages heavy with glossy photographs. She hesitated for a moment, then slowly pulled it onto her lap.

Flipping through the pages, she felt a pang of nostalgia – their wedding photos, their honeymoon in Greece, David's broad, easy smile as he held her hand on the white sands of Santorini. She turned another page, her eyes skimming over the images, and then she froze.

There it was – a photo from last Christmas. David, sitting beside the tree, a glass of wine in his hand, his head turned toward the camera, his eyes slightly narrowed against the flash.

She felt a chill creep down her spine.

She had taken that photo three months after his accident, three months after the doctors had declared him permanently blind.

She flipped to the next page, her heart hammering in her chest. Another photo, David in the backyard, his face tilted up toward the sun, his eyes closed, a faint, contented smile on his lips. She remembered that day clearly, it had been unusually warm for spring, the sun bright and unrelenting.

If he had been truly blind, why had he squinted?

Grace's hand trembled as she closed the album, her pulse pounding in her ears. She looked up, her gaze locking onto the back of David's head as he sat in his chair, his face turned toward the window, the morning sunlight casting a faint halo around him.

He was hiding something. She was sure of it now.

That afternoon, as Grace stepped outside to check the mailbox, she ran into Fiona. The older woman was pruning her rose bushes, her floral gardening gloves smeared with dirt, her face framed by a wide-brimmed sunhat.

"Morning, Grace," Fiona called, straightening up with a groan. "Lovely day, isn't it?"

Grace forced a smile, her mind still buzzing with questions. "Yes, beautiful. How are the roses coming along?"

"Oh, they're a handful, as always," Fiona chuckled, leaning on her gardening shears. "But I do love them."

Grace hesitated, her fingers brushing the cool metal of the mailbox. She glanced back at the house, her heart racing.

"Fiona," she said slowly, choosing her words carefully. "You've known David and me for years. You must have noticed... I mean, have you ever seen David... I don't know... do something that seemed... odd?"

Fiona's eyes narrowed slightly, her gaze sharpening. She glanced back at the house, then leaned in closer, lowering her voice.

"Funny you should ask," she whispered, glancing over her shoulder. "I did see something strange the other day. David was in the garden, and I swear, Grace, he turned his head when a bird landed on the fence. Like he heard it, or... saw it."

Grace felt her stomach drop, her heart pounding in her chest.

"He turned his head?" she whispered, her voice barely audible.

Fiona nodded, her eyes serious. "Yes. I thought I was imagining it, but now that you mention it... it did seem odd."

Grace forced a tight, strained smile, her heart racing as she turned back toward the house.

"Thank you, Fiona," she managed, her voice shaking. "I... I have to go."

As she hurried back inside, her mind whirling with this new piece of the puzzle, she felt a strange, icy determination settling over her.

David had secrets. And she was going to find out exactly what they were.

Grace spent the rest of the afternoon in a haze, her mind swirling with doubts and suspicions. She couldn't shake the feeling that something was deeply, profoundly wrong. David's accident had stolen his sight, or so she had believed. But now, every memory, every moment, every glance he had ever thrown in her direction felt like a clue she had missed.

That night, as they sat at the dinner table, Grace found herself watching David's every move. He reached for his glass with the same fluid, precise motion he always had, his fingers finding the thin stem without the slightest hesitation.

She chewed her food slowly, her mind racing. She had to know. She needed proof.

"David," she said, her voice carefully measured, "I was thinking... maybe we should redecorate the living room. It's been the same for years. Maybe a fresh look would do us some good."

David paused, his fork hovering in midair. He smiled, his face the picture of calm. "Sure, if you think so. I trust your judgment."

Grace forced a smile, her heart pounding. He was good, she had to admit. His tone was perfectly relaxed, his face unreadable. But she wasn't about to let him off the hook so easily.

The next morning, Grace rose early, her pulse quick with a mix of fear and determination. As David lingered over his morning coffee, she began the first phase of her test.

She shifted the armchair in the living room, moving it a few feet to the left. It was subtle, barely noticeable, but enough that someone walking through the room would need to adjust their path. She watched him carefully as he later made his way to his usual seat, his steps slow, deliberate.

He paused, his foot hesitating just slightly as he reached the new spot where the chair now stood. His hand reached out, fingers brushing the air before finding the armrest. He sank into the chair, his face still calm, but his jaw tightened for just a fraction of a second – a tiny, nearly imperceptible shift that Grace would have missed if she hadn't been watching so closely.

She felt a strange mix of satisfaction and fear twist in her stomach.

As the days passed, Grace became bolder. She swapped the mugs in the kitchen, moving his favorite one to the back of the cupboard. She rearranged the shoes by the front door, sliding his slippers to the opposite side of the rack. She even left the kitchen chair slightly pulled out, just enough to disrupt his usual, confident stride.

At first, David adapted quickly, his movements as fluid as ever. But over time, she noticed the small cracks in his routine. He hesitated more often, his steps less confident, his hands lingering on the edges of tables and countertops a little longer than usual.

Then, one evening, she deliberately left the TV remote on the far end of the coffee table, knowing he usually reached for it during his evening news program.

She watched from the kitchen, her heart racing as David reached for the remote, his hand moving confidently to the spot where it had always been. His fingers grasped empty air, his brow furrowing for just a fraction of a second before he casually adjusted, his hand sliding over the polished wood until it found the remote.

He leaned back, the tightness in his jaw visible even from across the room. Grace's pulse thundered in her ears.

He had reached for the remote as if he had known exactly where it should be. As if he had seen it.

That weekend, Grace took things a step further. She bought a small, decorative vase – bright red, impossible to miss – and placed it in the hallway, directly in David's usual path from the living room to the bedroom. She deliberately chose a day when she knew he would make the trip alone, late in the evening when the hallway was cast in deep, shadowed light.

She waited in the living room, her heart pounding, her ears straining for the sound of his footsteps.

A minute passed. Then another.

Finally, she heard him approach, his footsteps slow, cautious. She held her breath as he reached the hallway, his stride steady. For a split second, she braced herself for the sound of porcelain shattering against the hardwood floor.

But it never came.

Instead, she heard his footsteps pause, a slight rustling as he sidestepped the vase, his movements precise, deliberate.

Grace felt a cold wave of realization wash over her, her fingers tightening around the edge of the couch.

He had avoided the vase. Without touching it. Without knocking it over.

Without any warning that it was there.

Grace sat in the darkness long after David had gone to bed, her mind numb, her heart a wild, panicked beat in her chest. She felt the ground shift beneath her, her world tilting dangerously as she clutched the armrest, her breath coming in short, sharp gasps.

He could see.

David could see.

And he had been lying to her for months.

CHAPTER 5

The Mask Slips

The morning after the vase incident, Grace awoke with a tightness in her chest, a knot of dread that refused to untangle. She had barely slept, her mind replaying the moment David had stepped around the vase, his movements too deliberate, too precise for a man without sight.

As she padded into the kitchen, she found him already at the table, his hand wrapped around his coffee mug, his face calm, his expression perfectly composed.

"Morning," he said, his head tilting slightly in her direction. "Sleep well?"

Grace forced a smile, her heart hammering in her chest. "Yeah, just… just fine."

She poured herself a cup of tea, her hands trembling slightly as she reached for the kettle. She needed to stay calm, to think clearly. She couldn't confront him without more proof, without understanding the full extent of his deception.

That afternoon, Grace found herself outside, trimming the overgrown lavender bush by the front porch. She hadn't planned to be out there, but the steady rhythm of the garden shears and the crisp, cool air helped clear her mind.

"Grace!"

She looked up, her heart giving a little jolt as she saw Fiona shuffling down her driveway, her wide-brimmed sunhat casting a shadow over her wrinkled face.

"Morning, Fiona," Grace said, forcing a brightness into her voice that she didn't feel.

Fiona waddled over, leaning on her cane as she reached the edge of Grace's garden. She glanced back toward the house, her eyes narrowing slightly.

"I've been meaning to talk to you," she whispered, her voice dropping to a conspiratorial tone. "About David."

Grace's pulse quickened, her grip tightening on the shears. She felt a chill run down her spine.

"What about him?"

Fiona glanced around, as if worried the trees themselves might be listening. She leaned in closer, her breath smelling faintly of peppermint.

"I've been watching him," she said, her eyes sharp and calculating. "He's different, Grace. I've seen him moving around the garden, walking without his cane, turning his head toward the birds, bending down to pick up the mail without a second's hesitation."

Grace felt her knees go weak, the garden around her spinning slightly.

"Are you sure?" she whispered, her voice trembling.

Fiona straightened, her eyes bright with a mix of concern and intrigue. "Oh, I'm sure. And it's not just me. Dorothy from two houses down saw him watching the neighborhood kids playing soccer the other afternoon. Said his head followed the ball like a hawk."

Grace felt the world tilt beneath her feet, her pulse a wild, erratic beat in her chest. She forced herself to take a deep breath, to steady her shaking hands.

"I... I don't know what to say," she stammered, her mind racing.

Fiona reached out, placing a bony hand on Grace's arm, her grip surprisingly strong.

"Just keep your eyes open, dear," she whispered, her eyes dark and serious. "Sometimes, the people closest to us can be the ones hiding the darkest secrets."

That evening, Grace sat across from David at the dinner table, her mind still reeling from her conversation with Fiona. She watched him carefully, every movement, every gesture, every flicker of his eyelids.

"David," she said suddenly, her voice sharper than she intended. "I was thinking, maybe we should visit my sister next weekend. It's been a while."

David paused, his fork halfway to his mouth. His jaw tightened, just for a second, before he forced a smile.

"That sounds nice," he said, his tone even, his expression perfectly composed.

Grace felt a cold wave of doubt wash over her. She had hoped for a reaction, a slip, anything to confirm her suspicions. But David's mask held firm, his face a picture of calm, his movements smooth and confident.

Later that night, as David showered, Grace found herself in his study, the small, cluttered room that had become his sanctuary since the accident. She hesitated for a moment, her heart racing, before pushing the door open and stepping inside.

The room smelled faintly of aftershave and old paper, the air heavy with the scent of leather-bound books and polished wood. She moved slowly, her eyes scanning the shelves, the desk, the neat stacks of papers and notebooks.

Her heart nearly stopped when she spotted it, a pair of sunglasses, the expensive, polarized kind that golfers and sailors wore, resting on the corner of his desk.

She reached out, her fingers trembling as she lifted them, turning them over in her hands. The lenses were spotless, the frames polished, the soft rubber nose pads free of dust.

Why would a blind man need polarized sunglasses?

She felt her stomach twist, her breath coming in short, shallow gasps.

David was lying to her. She was sure of it now. But why?

She placed the sunglasses back on the desk, her mind spinning, her heart racing. She had to find out the truth. She had to confront him. But how?

As she stepped back, her hand brushed against a small, leather-bound notebook lying open beside the sunglasses. She froze, her eyes locking onto the page.

The handwriting was David's, neat, precise, each letter perfectly formed. She leaned in, her pulse pounding in her ears as she read the words scribbled across the page:

"Remember to keep up the act. Eyes down. Don't look too confident. Keep the mask on."

Grace staggered back, her breath catching in her throat.

The mask.

The mask.

Her world tilted, the room spinning around her as she clutched the edge of the desk for support.

David was not just hiding his sight. He was playing a role, a carefully constructed lie, a deception that reached far deeper than she had ever imagined.

And she had no idea why.

Grace felt like a ghost in her own home, moving silently through the rooms, her heart heavy with the burden of suspicion. The sunglasses, the notebook, and Fiona's whispers had planted a seed of doubt so deep that it twisted her thoughts, making her question every word, every gesture, every breath David took.

She had tried to ignore it, to push the doubts aside, to tell herself that she was being paranoid. But the evidence was piling up, and she could no longer deny it.

David was hiding something.

The following morning, Grace shuffled into the kitchen, her eyes tired, her mind still spinning from the sleepless night. She found David standing by the sink, his head tilted slightly as if listening to the distant call of a bird outside the window.

"Morning," he said, his voice warm, too warm, as if sensing her presence before she had made a sound.

Grace's heart skipped a beat. She glanced at his face, at the slight turn of his head, the way his eyes seemed to track her as she moved toward the fridge.

"Morning," she replied, her voice tight, her hands shaking as she poured herself a cup of coffee.

David stepped back from the sink, moving with a fluid, confident grace that made her stomach churn. She watched him carefully as he reached for his cup on the counter, his fingers finding it with a precision that felt too perfect, too deliberate.

As he brought the cup to his lips, Grace took a deep breath, her heart racing. She needed to test him, to see if he would slip.

"David," she said, trying to keep her voice casual, "do you remember that old oak tree we used to sit under at the park? The one near the fountain?"

David paused for a fraction of a second, his cup hovering just below his mouth. Grace saw the muscles in his jaw tighten, his eyes flicker ever so slightly.

"Of course," he said, his voice steady but his grip tightening on the cup. "How could I forget?"

Grace's pulse quickened. She forced a smile, her mind racing. How could a blind man remember the location of a tree, the position of a fountain?

Later that day, as Grace sat in the living room, staring blankly at the wall, the doorbell rang, startling her out of her thoughts. She stood up, her heart pounding as she moved to the door, her mind still spinning with doubts.

She opened the door to find Fiona standing on the porch, her sharp eyes glittering, her thin lips pulled into a tight line.

"Fiona," Grace said, forcing a smile. "What brings you here?"

Fiona stepped forward, leaning on her cane as she glanced over Grace's shoulder into the house.

"I needed to talk to you," she whispered, her voice low and urgent. "May I come in?"

Grace hesitated for a moment before stepping aside, waving the older woman in. Fiona shuffled past her, her eyes darting around the room, her nose twitching like a bloodhound on the scent of something foul.

They settled in the living room, Fiona perching on the edge of the couch, her eyes never leaving Grace's face.

"I've been thinking about our conversation the other day," Fiona began, her voice dropping to a whisper. "About David."

Grace's heart tightened, her breath catching in her throat.

"What about him?" she whispered, her fingers digging into the armrest.

Fiona leaned in, her eyes narrowing. "I saw him again yesterday, walking down the garden path, his head up, his steps sure and confident."

Grace felt the blood drain from her face, her pulse pounding in her ears.

"He looked straight at me, Grace," Fiona continued, her voice shaking slightly. "Not past me, not toward me – at me. His eyes met mine, and for a moment, I swear I saw a flicker of recognition."

Grace felt her hands tremble, her heart thundering in her chest. She opened her mouth to respond, but no words came out.

"I don't know what he's playing at," Fiona whispered, her fingers tightening on the head of her cane. "But I'm telling you, there's more to this than we thought."

That evening, as the house settled into its usual quiet, Grace found herself standing outside David's study, her heart racing, her mind a chaotic swirl of anger and confusion.

She pushed the door open, stepping into the small, cluttered room, her eyes locking onto David as he sat at his desk, his head bent over a stack of papers.

"David," she said, her voice sharp, her chest tight with a mixture of fear and fury.

David's head snapped up, his eyes wide, his hands freezing on the desk. For a split second, Grace saw the fear in his eyes, the panic that flashed across his face before he forced a calm, blank expression.

"What is it?" he asked, his voice steady but his fingers trembling slightly.

Grace took a step forward, her fists clenched, her breath coming in short, ragged gasps.

"I know," she whispered, her voice breaking, tears stinging her eyes. "I know you've been lying to me."

David's face paled, his mouth opening and closing like a fish out of water, his hands clenching into fists on the desk.

"I don't know what you're talking about," he stammered, his voice shaking.

Grace took another step forward, her heart pounding, her vision blurring with tears.

"Stop lying to me!" she cried, her voice echoing off the walls, her fists trembling at her sides. "I know you can see, David. I know you've been faking it this whole time."

David froze, his body going rigid, his eyes locked onto hers, his mouth set in a thin, grim line.

For a long, terrible moment, neither of them spoke, the air between them crackling with unspoken words, with betrayal and fear and a hundred other emotions that neither of them dared to name.

Then, slowly, David leaned back in his chair, his eyes never leaving Grace's face.

"I can explain," he whispered, his voice hollow, his eyes dark and unreadable.

Grace felt her knees go weak, her heart shattering in her chest.

"You'd better," she whispered, her voice shaking, her hands clenching into fists at her sides. "Because right now, I don't know who you are anymore."

CHAPTER 6

Ghosts in the Mirror

Grace felt like the walls of her home were closing in, the air thick with secrets, lies, and betrayal. The confrontation with David had left her shaken, her mind reeling, her heart shattered into a thousand pieces.

As she stumbled out of his study, her breaths coming in short, panicked gasps, her mind began to unravel the past, piecing together every odd glance, every misplaced step, every suspicious whisper.

It was a warm spring afternoon, the air heavy with the scent of freshly cut grass and blooming roses. Grace had thrown a garden party to celebrate their tenth wedding anniversary, inviting friends, family, and neighbors.

David had been in high spirits that day, his laughter echoing across the garden as he moved gracefully among the guests, his hand on her arm, his head tilted as if listening to the distant chatter.

Fiona had been there too, her sharp eyes never leaving David's face as he moved through the crowd, his steps confident, his head turning toward the clinking of glasses, the rustle of dresses, the low hum of conversation.

At one point, Grace had caught a strange look on Fiona's face – a mixture of confusion and suspicion – as David had bent down to pick up a fallen napkin with an ease that seemed too practiced, too precise for a blind man.

"Your husband has good instincts," Fiona had whispered to Grace later that evening, her eyes narrowing as she watched David laugh with a group of old friends near the bar. "Almost as if he can see the world around him."

Grace had laughed off the comment at the time, brushing it aside as one of Fiona's many quirks. But now, the memory stabbed at her heart, twisting the knife of betrayal deeper into her soul.

As Grace stumbled up the stairs, her mind racing, she heard the creak of the front door opening behind her. She spun around, her heart pounding, expecting to see David emerging from his study. But instead, she found herself staring at a tall, sharply dressed man with salt-and-pepper hair and a thin, angular face. His eyes were dark, almost black, and they locked onto hers with an intensity that made her blood run cold.

"Grace," the man said, his voice deep and smooth, his lips curling into a thin, predatory smile.

Grace's hand flew to her chest, her pulse thundering in her ears.

"Who... who are you?" she stammered, her back pressing against the banister, her fingers tightening around the cold wood.

The man stepped into the hallway, closing the door behind him with a soft click, his eyes never leaving hers.

"My name is Dr. Richard Wallace," he said, his voice calm, his eyes dark and unreadable. "I'm an old... friend of David's."

Grace felt her knees go weak, her breath catching in her throat.

"What... what are you doing here?" she whispered, her heart racing, her mind spinning with a thousand unanswered questions.

Dr. Wallace smiled, his eyes flicking to the study door behind her.

"I think it's time we had a little chat," he said, his voice dropping to a whisper, his eyes narrowing as he took a step closer. "About your husband... and the secrets he's been keeping from you."

Grace's mind flashed back to a memory she had long buried, a moment from five years earlier, when she had accompanied David to a medical conference in Sydney.

David had been a keynote speaker, his voice confident and commanding as he addressed the crowd of surgeons, doctors, and medical researchers. She had sat in the front row, her heart swelling with pride as she listened to him speak, his voice echoing through the grand, high-ceilinged hall.

After the speech, a tall, thin man with dark eyes and a sharp jawline had approached them, his hand extended, his smile cold and calculating.

"Dr. Wallace," he had said, his eyes flicking to David's face with a strange, knowing look. "It's been too long."

David's face had tightened, his jaw clenching, his eyes narrowing as he reached out to shake the man's hand.

"Yes," he had replied, his voice strained, his grip firm. "Far too long."

Grace had felt a chill run down her spine, her heart tightening as she watched the two men exchange a long, silent glance, their eyes locked, their bodies tense.

Dr. Wallace took another step toward Grace, his eyes glinting with a dangerous light, his lips curling into a thin, twisted smile. "You don't know your husband at all, do you, Grace?" he whispered, his voice dripping with malice, his eyes narrowing as he leaned in closer.

Grace felt her blood run cold, her pulse thundering in her ears.

"What... what do you mean?" she stammered, her fingers digging into the banister, her heart racing, her mind spinning with fear and confusion.

Dr. Wallace leaned in, his lips inches from her ear, his breath hot against her skin.

"I know his secret," he whispered, his voice low and menacing, his eyes dark and piercing. "And if you're not careful, it will destroy you both."

Grace felt her knees give way, her breath catching in her throat, her mind shattering into a thousand pieces as the world around her spun into darkness.

David sat in his study, his fingers tapping rhythmically on the polished mahogany desk. The air around him felt thicker than usual, the shadows longer, the silence more pronounced. He had felt it, that familiar prickle at the back of his neck, ever since he heard the door click shut downstairs.

He straightened, his eyes narrowing behind the thick glasses that concealed his sharp, calculating gaze. He heard Grace's hurried footsteps on the stairs, the panicked creak of the banister as she backed away, her sharp, fearful voice cutting through the silence.

Then, the low, rumbling chuckle of a man he had hoped never to see again.

Dr. Richard Wallace.

David's heart clenched, his mind racing. He had known this day might come, but not like this, not when he was so close to pulling off the ultimate deception.

The study door creaked open slowly, and David's entire body tensed, his muscles coiling like a snake preparing to strike.

"David," Wallace's voice cut through the thick air like a blade, dripping with dark amusement. "Still hiding behind those glasses, I see."

David felt a cold wave of dread wash over him, his mind flashing back to the last time he had faced this man, the medical conference in Sydney, the tense handshake, the knowing glances.

David forced a smile, leaning back in his leather chair, his fingers tightening around the carved wooden armrests.

"Richard," he said, his voice calm, almost dismissive. "To what do I owe the pleasure?"

Wallace stepped into the room, his tall, thin frame cutting a sharp silhouette against the dimly lit hallway. He closed the door behind him, his eyes never leaving David's face.

"Oh, I just thought it was time for a little reunion," Wallace said, his lips curling into a wicked smile, his eyes glinting with dangerous intent. "After all, we have so much to catch up on."

David clenched his jaw, his fingers flexing on the armrests. He felt the heat rising in his chest, the familiar burn of anger and fear mingling in his veins.

"I didn't invite you into my home, Richard," David said, his voice low and steady, his eyes narrowing behind his glasses. "And I'm not in the mood for games."

Wallace let out a short, mocking laugh, his head tilting as he stepped closer, his polished leather shoes sinking into the thick carpet.

"Oh, come now, David," he said, his voice dripping with condescension. "You of all people should appreciate the art of deception. After all, you've become quite the master of it."

David's heart pounded in his chest, his mind racing as he calculated his next move, his fingers tightening around the wooden armrests until his knuckles turned white.

"What do you want, Richard?" David hissed, his voice sharp and venomous, his eyes locking onto Wallace's dark, predatory gaze.

Wallace smirked, his eyes flicking to the darkened windows, the shadows dancing across the polished wood of the study walls.

"I want what I've always wanted," he said, his voice low and dangerous, his eyes narrowing as he took another step forward. "Control."

David felt a chill run down his spine, his mind flashing back to the early days of their partnership, the long nights in the lab, the whispered conversations over whiskey and dim lights, the promises of power and influence.

He had broken free from Wallace's grip years ago, severing ties, cutting the strings that had bound him to the dark, twisted world of medical experimentation and deceit.

But Wallace had never truly let him go.

"You don't scare me, Richard," David spat, his voice dripping with defiance, his eyes blazing behind the thick, tinted lenses.

Wallace's smile widened, his eyes glinting with a twisted delight, his long, thin fingers drumming lightly on the edge of David's desk.

"Oh, but I should," he whispered, leaning in closer, his breath hot against David's ear. "Because I know your secret... and I can bring it all crashing down."

David felt his pulse quicken, his breath catching in his throat, his mind spinning as he calculated the odds, his body tensing for a fight.

"What do you want?" David growled, his teeth clenched, his muscles coiling like a spring ready to snap.

Wallace straightened, his eyes dark and cold, his lips curling into a thin, twisted smile.

"I want my piece of the pie," he said, his voice dripping with venom, his eyes narrowing as he leaned in closer. "And if you refuse, I'll make sure your precious little wife learns the truth about you... and your miraculous recovery."

David felt the blood drain from his face, his heart thundering in his chest, his mind shattering into a thousand pieces as the full weight of Wallace's threat crashed down upon him.

"You wouldn't dare," David whispered, his voice trembling with fear and rage, his eyes narrowing behind the thick, dark lenses.

Wallace straightened, his smile widening, his eyes glinting with a dark, twisted delight.

"Try me," he whispered, his voice low and menacing, his eyes locked onto David's pale, trembling face. "And watch your world burn."

With that, Wallace turned on his heel, his polished shoes clicking softly against the thick carpet as he strode toward the door, his dark, mocking laughter echoing through the dimly lit study.

David sat frozen in his chair, his mind spinning, his heart racing, his entire world on the brink of collapse.

CHAPTER 7

Shadows and Suspicions

Grace barely slept that night. Her mind raced, replaying the hushed, sinister conversation between David and the stranger — Richard. Every creak of the house, every rustle of the wind outside seemed to carry a hidden threat, an unspoken danger lurking just beyond her reach.

The morning light crept through the heavy bedroom curtains, casting long, thin shadows across the quilted bedspread. David lay beside her, his breathing deep and steady, his face calm and untroubled. She stared at him, her mind spinning, trying to reconcile the man beside her with the fearful, cornered voice she had overheard just hours earlier.

What had he meant by miraculous recovery?

Grace slipped quietly from the bed, her bare feet brushing against the cool wooden floor. She wrapped her robe tightly around herself, the thick, warm fabric a small comfort against the chill creeping into her bones. She padded down the hallway, her heart still pounding in her chest, and gently pushed open the door to David's study.

The air inside was stale and heavy, tinged with the faint, bitter scent of whiskey and the smoky residue of the Cuban cigars David kept locked in the bottom drawer of his desk. She glanced around, her eyes scanning the tidy bookshelves, the perfectly arranged papers, the neat, orderly rows of file folders.

She hesitated for a moment, her fingers hovering over the polished surface of the desk, before slowly pulling open the top drawer. It slid out smoothly, revealing a neat array of pens, sticky notes, and paper clips, perfectly arranged in little compartments. She moved to the next drawer, her pulse quickening as she slowly eased it open.

The contents were more chaotic – stacks of letters, unopened bills, a small, locked black box that sent a fresh jolt of suspicion through her veins. She reached for it, her fingers trembling slightly as she tried to lift it, but it was heavy and cold, the tiny silver lock glinting up at her like a silent, mocking eye.

She placed it back carefully, closing the drawer just as she heard the soft creak of the floorboards behind her.

"Grace?"

She spun around, her heart slamming against her ribs as David appeared in the doorway, his dark eyes narrowing slightly as he took in the scene.

"What are you doing in my study?" he asked, his voice calm but edged with a sharpness that sent a fresh wave of anxiety crashing over her.

She forced a small, shaky smile, quickly pulling her robe tighter around herself.

"Oh, I was just... just looking for the power bill. It's come due, and I thought I might sort it out before breakfast," she replied, her voice barely steady.

David's eyes lingered on her for a long, tense moment, his dark gaze flicking from her trembling fingers to the half-open drawer beside her.

"I'll handle that," he said, his voice firm, his eyes never leaving hers. "You don't need to worry about it."

He stepped forward, gently but firmly guiding her out of the study, his large hand resting heavily on her shoulder as he pulled the door shut behind them.

Grace's heart raced, her mind whirling with a thousand unanswered questions as she felt the subtle, unmistakable shift in the atmosphere between them. For the first time in years, she felt like a stranger in her own home, a silent, unwelcome intruder in the carefully curated world David had built around them.

Later that day, as she stood at the kitchen sink, scrubbing the breakfast dishes with a fierce, nervous energy, the doorbell rang. She froze, her hands dripping with soapy water, her mind still tangled with doubts and suspicions.

She quickly dried her hands on a dish towel, her heart pounding as she hurried to the front door.

It was Anna, their nosey neighbor, her sharp, watchful eyes gleaming with curiosity as she leaned casually against the doorframe.

"Grace, darling!" Anna sang out, her red lipstick bright against her pale skin, her carefully styled hair glinting in the morning sun. "I was just popping by to see how you're holding up. I heard about David's accident... and I must say, it's a miracle he's doing so well now. You must be so relieved!"

Grace's heart skipped a beat, her mind flashing back to the whispered threats and sinister warnings she had overheard the night before. She forced a strained, tight-lipped smile, gripping the doorframe with whitening knuckles.

"Oh... yes, he's... he's doing much better, thank you," she replied, her voice hollow, her eyes flicking nervously back towards the hallway, half expecting David to appear at any moment.

Anna leaned in closer, her eyes narrowing slightly as she dropped her voice to a conspiratorial whisper.

"Though, I must admit, he's looking much too fit for a man who just came back from the brink of death. I mean, just yesterday I saw him walking down the street with a confidence I haven't seen in years. It's almost like he's a different person entirely..."

Grace's heart thudded painfully in her chest, her breath catching in her throat as Anna's words echoed in her mind.

Almost like a different person entirely...

Anna flashed her a quick, sharp smile, her eyes gleaming with the thrill of fresh gossip as she straightened up and adjusted her sunglasses.

"Well, I won't keep you, darling. I'm sure you have a million things to do. But do let me know if you ever need someone to talk to... or if you ever want to, you know, share a little secret."

With that, she turned on her heel, her heels clicking sharply against the front porch as she sauntered back towards her immaculate, rose-covered garden.

Grace closed the door slowly, her mind reeling, her fingers trembling as she leaned heavily against the polished wood.

What was happening? What was David hiding from her?

Grace sat at the kitchen table, the morning sun casting long, trembling shadows through the lace curtains. Her coffee had gone cold, the thin steam long since faded, but she hadn't moved for the past half hour. Anna's words still echoed in her mind, each syllable a tiny hammer tapping against the fragile glass of her sanity.

"Almost like a different person entirely..."

The phrase twisted in her mind, mingling with the whispered threats she had overheard, the sinister undertone in David's voice as he had spoken to that stranger – Richard. She felt her pulse quicken, her hands clenching into tight fists on the tabletop.

What was happening?

That afternoon, Grace forced herself to leave the house. She needed fresh air, needed to clear her mind before the creeping paranoia swallowed her whole. She pulled on her coat, grabbing her handbag with shaking hands, and stepped out onto the cracked, sun-warmed sidewalk.

As she turned onto the main road, her mind still spinning, she nearly collided with Sam, the middle-aged postman who had been delivering their mail for years.

"Morning, Mrs. Gallagher!" Sam greeted her with a wide, friendly grin, his sun-weathered face crinkling at the corners. He adjusted his cap, his blue uniform crisp and neat despite the rising summer heat.

"Morning, Sam," she replied, forcing a small, tight smile.

"Good to see you out and about," he said, leaning slightly on his bicycle, the metal frame creaking under his weight. "I saw David jogging the other day – looking quite fit for a man who just had a major accident. Must be a miracle recovery, eh?"

Grace's heart skipped a beat, her mind flashing back to Anna's whispered words, the sharp, knowing gleam in her eyes.

"Oh, yes," Grace replied, her voice tight, her pulse racing. "It's... it's truly remarkable."

Sam nodded, oblivious to the storm of doubt brewing behind her forced smile.

"Well, you two take care now. It's good to see the Gallaghers back on their feet," he said, giving her a small, cheerful wave before pedaling off down the street, his whistle carrying back to her on the warm summer breeze.

Grace stood frozen on the sidewalk, her mind racing, the cracks in the pavement beneath her feet seeming to widen and shift, threatening to swallow her whole.

Later that evening, Grace found herself standing at the kitchen counter, her hands moving automatically as she chopped vegetables for dinner. The rhythmic *thunk-thunk-thunk* of the knife against the cutting board was almost hypnotic, a steady, comforting beat that momentarily drowned out the chaos in her mind.

David walked in, his footsteps slow and deliberate, his presence filling the small, sunlit kitchen with a sudden, stifling tension. He paused in the doorway, his dark eyes fixing on her with a curious, unreadable intensity.

"Grace," he said, his voice low and careful. "You've been... distant lately. Is everything alright?"

She felt her hand tighten around the knife handle, the cool, polished wood pressing into her palm. She forced herself to meet his gaze, her heart pounding, her mind racing with a thousand unspoken questions.

Should she confront him? Should she demand the truth?

"Oh, I'm fine," she replied, her voice trembling slightly. "Just... tired, I suppose."

David stepped closer, his shadow falling across the countertop, his eyes narrowing slightly as he reached for the freshly chopped carrots, popping one into his mouth with a slow, thoughtful chew.

"You know," he said, his tone casual but his eyes sharp, watchful, "you can talk to me, Grace. You don't have to carry everything on your own."

She forced a thin, brittle smile, her pulse racing as she felt his gaze linger on her face, as if searching for something hidden behind her wide, fearful eyes.

"I know," she whispered, her fingers trembling against the cold, polished handle of the knife.

David leaned in, his breath warm against her cheek, his hand resting lightly on her shoulder.

"Good," he murmured, his voice dropping to a low, almost threatening whisper. "Because secrets... have a way of eating you alive."

Grace felt a sharp, icy shiver run down her spine, her heart slamming against her ribs as David slowly straightened, his dark eyes never leaving her face as he turned and walked out of the kitchen, his footsteps echoing down the hallway like the slow, measured toll of a funeral bell.

That night, Grace lay awake in the dark, the steady, rhythmic rise and fall of David's breathing beside her a constant, suffocating reminder of the widening chasm between them.

She felt trapped, cornered, her mind spinning, her heart aching with a terrible, unspoken fear.

What had she stumbled into? What dark, twisted secret was David hiding from her?

And more importantly...

What would he do if he found out she knew?

CHAPTER 8

Shadows in the Light

Grace sat at the kitchen table, her mind churning like the dark waters of a storm-tossed sea. The morning light slanted through the windows, casting long, jagged shadows that seemed to reach for her, as if the house itself was conspiring against her sanity.

She had been replaying David's words from the night before over and over in her mind, his sharp, almost threatening whisper still echoing in her ears.

"Secrets... have a way of eating you alive."

She shivered, her fingers clenching around the warm, ceramic mug in her hands, the rich, bitter aroma of her morning coffee doing little to soothe her frayed nerves.

Outside, the neighborhood was slowly waking up, the distant hum of car engines and the cheerful chatter of early morning dog walkers filtering through the thin walls of the old house. Grace glanced out the window, her gaze catching on the bright yellow house across the street, where Anna was already out in her garden, her lean, athletic frame bending and stretching as she pruned her rose bushes with quick, practiced snips.

Grace's mind flashed back to her last conversation with Anna, the unsettling gleam in her neighbor's eyes, the pointed, knowing tone of her voice. *"Almost like a different person entirely..."*

She felt her pulse quicken, her mind racing as a dark, unsettling thought began to take shape in the back of her mind.

What if Anna knew something? What if she had seen something... something Grace had missed?

An hour later, Grace found herself standing on Anna's doorstep, her heart racing, her mind spinning with a thousand unspoken fears. She hesitated for a moment, her hand hovering over the shiny brass knocker, before finally letting it fall with a sharp, decisive rap.

The door swung open almost immediately, revealing Anna's bright, curious face, her sharp blue eyes lighting up with a spark of surprise.

"Grace! What a pleasant surprise," Anna said, stepping aside to let her neighbor in. "Come in, come in."

Grace stepped into the cool, shadowed hallway, the faint, sweet scent of lavender and freshly cut flowers hanging in the air, mingling with the warm, comforting aroma of freshly brewed tea.

"Thank you," Grace murmured, her hands twisting nervously in front of her as Anna led her into the cozy, sunlit living room.

They settled into the plush, overstuffed armchairs by the large bay window, the thin, gauzy curtains billowing gently in the warm morning breeze. Anna poured them both a cup of tea, her movements quick and graceful, her sharp, watchful eyes never leaving Grace's face.

"To what do I owe the pleasure?" Anna asked, her tone light but her gaze sharp, probing.

Grace hesitated, her heart pounding, her fingers tightening around the warm, delicate porcelain of her teacup.

"I just... I've been thinking," she began slowly, her voice trembling slightly. "About what you said the other day. About David... about how he seems... different."

Anna's sharp blue eyes flickered, a small, almost imperceptible smile tugging at the corners of her lips.

"Oh?" she said, leaning in slightly, her tone low and conspiratorial. "Go on."

Grace took a deep breath, her mind racing, her pulse thundering in her ears.

"I just... I can't shake the feeling that something is... off," she whispered, her eyes flicking nervously towards the door, as if expecting David to burst in at any moment, his dark eyes flashing with rage.

Anna's smile widened, her sharp, manicured nails tapping lightly against the delicate porcelain of her teacup.

"Well," she said, her voice dropping to a low, almost conspiratorial whisper, "you're not the only one who's noticed."

Grace felt her heart skip a beat, her pulse racing as Anna leaned in closer, her sharp, watchful eyes glittering with a strange, unsettling intensity.

"There's something I've been meaning to tell you," Anna continued, her voice low and urgent. "Something I probably should have mentioned before... but I didn't want to worry you."

Grace felt a cold, sharp knot of fear twist in her stomach, her mind spinning with a thousand dark, terrible possibilities.

"What... what is it?" she whispered, her voice trembling.

Anna hesitated for a moment, her sharp blue eyes flicking towards the door, as if fearing they might be overheard, before finally leaning in even closer, her breath warm against Grace's ear.

"About a month ago," Anna whispered, her voice low and tense, "I saw David... in the garden. Late at night, around midnight. He was... digging."

Grace felt her heart stop, her mind going blank, her hands clenching tightly around the delicate, trembling porcelain of her teacup.

"Digging?" she whispered, her voice barely audible.

Anna nodded, her sharp, manicured nails tapping lightly against the delicate porcelain, her eyes glittering with a strange, almost gleeful intensity.

"Yes," she whispered, her voice dropping to a low, almost sinister hiss. "And not just once... but every night for almost a week."

Grace felt her heart lurch, her mind spinning, her pulse thundering in her ears as a thousand dark, terrible possibilities raced through her mind.

What had David buried in their garden? And why had he kept it a secret?

Grace felt like she was floating, her mind a chaotic swirl of fear, confusion, and disbelief as she stumbled back across the street to her house. Anna's words echoed in her mind, her sharp, whispered confession cutting through the thick fog of denial that had been clouding Grace's thoughts for weeks.

"He was digging... every night for almost a week."

The words replayed in her head like a twisted, broken record, the sharp, metallic clink of Anna's teacup against the saucer still ringing in her ears. She felt like she was trapped in a nightmare, her every step heavy and unsteady, her breath coming in short, shallow gasps as she fumbled for her keys, her trembling fingers barely able to fit the small, jagged metal into the lock.

The door swung open, the familiar, comforting scent of their home washing over her in a wave of bitter nostalgia. She stumbled into the hallway, her heart racing, her mind spinning, her every nerve tingling with a dark, terrible anticipation.

David was in the living room, his tall, lean frame hunched over the small, battered workbench he had set up by the window, his strong, calloused hands expertly piecing together the delicate, intricate parts of an old pocket watch he had been restoring for weeks.

He looked up as she entered, his dark, piercing eyes locking onto hers for a brief, heart-stopping moment, a small, knowing smile flickering at the corners of his lips.

"Grace," he said, his deep, gravelly voice calm and measured, his sharp, watchful eyes never leaving her face. "You're back early."

Grace felt her breath catch in her throat, her heart pounding, her mind racing with a thousand dark, terrible possibilities as she forced herself to meet his gaze, her pulse thundering in her ears. "Yeah... Anna just needed a bit of company," she replied, forcing a thin, strained smile onto her trembling lips. "You know how she gets."

David's dark eyes flickered, a small, almost imperceptible smile tugging at the corners of his mouth as he carefully set the small, delicate watch parts down on the workbench, his sharp, calloused fingers moving with a strange, almost mechanical precision.

"Of course," he said, his voice low and smooth, his sharp, watchful eyes still locked onto hers. "Anna's always been a bit... lonely."

Grace felt her pulse quicken, her mind spinning, her every nerve tingling with a dark, terrible anticipation as she forced herself to turn away, her heart racing, her breath coming in short, shallow gasps as she stumbled into the kitchen, her trembling fingers fumbling with the kettle as she tried to steady her nerves.

As the water boiled, she found herself staring out the small, fogged-up kitchen window, her eyes locking onto the small, overgrown patch of garden just outside, the thick, tangled vines and wild, untamed bushes casting long, jagged shadows across the dark, uneven soil.

She felt a cold, sharp knot of fear twist in her stomach, her mind racing, her pulse thundering in her ears as she tried to piece together the dark, twisted puzzle that her life had become.

What had David buried out there? And why had he kept it a secret?

She felt her heart lurch, her breath catching in her throat as a dark, terrible thought crossed her mind, her sharp, panicked gasp echoing through the small, empty kitchen.

What if he had buried more than just his secrets?

That night, as the shadows deepened and the cool, crisp autumn air settled over the house, Grace found herself standing at the small, battered garden shed, her trembling fingers clutching the cold, rusted metal handle of an old, battered shovel, her mind racing, her pulse thundering in her ears as she forced herself to step out into the cool, dark night.

The small, overgrown patch of garden loomed ahead, its thick, tangled vines and wild, untamed bushes casting long, jagged shadows across the dark, uneven soil, the faint, metallic clink of the shovel against the hard, compacted earth echoing through the still, silent night.

She dug for what felt like hours, her every muscle aching, her breath coming in short, sharp gasps as she forced the cold, rusted metal deeper and deeper into the thick, compacted soil, the sharp, metallic clink of the shovel against the hard, unyielding earth ringing in her ears like the slow, steady tolling of a funeral bell.

And then, finally, her shovel hit something hard.

She froze, her heart racing, her mind spinning, her every nerve tingling with a dark, terrible anticipation as she carefully scraped away the thick, compacted soil, her trembling fingers brushing against the cold, hard surface of...

A small, battered metal box.

She felt her breath catch in her throat, her heart pounding, her pulse thundering in her ears as she carefully pried the small, rusted lid open, her sharp, panicked gasp echoing through the dark, empty garden as she stared down at the small, delicate contents of the box, her mind spinning, her every nerve tingling with a dark, terrible realization.

Inside, wrapped in a thin, blood-stained cloth, were a pair of broken, shattered eyeglasses, their thick, scratched lenses gleaming in the faint, silvery moonlight, their thin, twisted metal frames bent and warped, as if crushed under the weight of a terrible, unspeakable force.

She stumbled back, her trembling fingers clenching around the cold, rusted handle of the shovel, her mind spinning, her pulse thundering in her ears as she stared down at the small, battered metal box, her heart racing, her breath coming in short, sharp gasps as a dark, terrible realization settled over her like a thick, suffocating fog.

David's old glasses. The ones he had worn before the accident.

The ones he had supposedly thrown away.

Grace felt her knees buckle, her vision blurring, her mind spinning as she stumbled back towards the house, her heart racing, her breath coming in short, sharp gasps as she tried to process the dark, terrible truth that had just been unearthed in their own backyard.

David had been lying to her... all along.

CHAPTER 9

Confrontation

Grace's mind raced, her heart pounding, her breath coming in short, sharp gasps as she stumbled back into the house, her trembling fingers still clutching the cold, rusted handle of the old, battered shovel. She felt like she was floating, her every nerve tingling with a dark, terrible anticipation as she forced herself to step into the small, dimly lit hallway, the sharp, metallic clink of the shovel against the wooden floor echoing through the silent, empty house.

David was still in the living room, his tall, lean frame hunched over the small, battered workbench by the window, his sharp, calloused fingers moving with a strange, mechanical precision as he carefully pieced together the delicate, intricate parts of an old pocket watch.

He didn't look up as she entered, his dark, piercing eyes locked onto the small, delicate gears and springs scattered across the battered wooden surface, his strong, angular jaw clenched, his sharp, calloused fingers moving with a cold, calculated precision that sent a sharp, icy shiver down Grace's spine.

She felt her breath catch in her throat, her heart racing, her pulse thundering in her ears as she took a small, hesitant step forward, the sharp, metallic clink of the shovel against the wooden floor ringing in her ears like the slow, steady tolling of a funeral bell.

"David," she said, her voice low and shaky, her trembling fingers clenching around the cold, rusted metal of the shovel handle as she forced herself to meet his sharp, watchful gaze. "We need to talk."

David's dark, piercing eyes flicked up, locking onto hers for a brief, heart-stopping moment, a small, knowing smile flickering at the corners of his mouth as he carefully set the small, delicate watch parts down on the workbench, his sharp, calloused fingers still for the first time in what felt like hours.

"Grace," he said, his deep, gravelly voice calm and measured, his sharp, watchful eyes never leaving her face. "Is something wrong?"

Grace felt her heart lurch, her mind spinning, her every nerve tingling with a dark, terrible anticipation as she took another small, hesitant step forward, her pulse thundering in her ears, her breath coming in short, shallow gasps as she carefully set the old, battered shovel down on the small, wooden table by the door.

"Where are your old glasses, David?" she asked, her voice low and trembling, her sharp, panicked breath echoing through the small, dimly lit hallway as she forced herself to meet his dark, piercing gaze.

David's sharp, watchful eyes flickered, his tall, lean frame stiffening for a brief, heart-stopping moment as he carefully rose to his feet, his sharp, calloused fingers clenching into tight, white-knuckled fists at his sides, his dark, piercing eyes still locked onto hers.

"I told you, Grace," he said, his deep, gravelly voice low and measured, his sharp, watchful eyes never leaving her face. "I threw them away... months ago."

Grace felt a cold, sharp knot of fear twist in her stomach, her mind racing, her pulse thundering in her ears as she took another small, hesitant step forward, her trembling fingers clenching around the cold, rusted metal of the shovel handle as she forced herself to hold his sharp, watchful gaze.

"You're lying," she whispered, her voice low and trembling, her sharp, panicked breath echoing through the small, dimly lit hallway as she carefully pulled the small, battered metal box from the deep, hidden pocket of her jacket, her trembling fingers carefully prying the thin, rusted lid open as she held it out for him to see.

David's dark, piercing eyes flicked down, locking onto the small, blood-stained cloth wrapped around the shattered, broken eyeglasses inside, his sharp, calloused fingers clenching into tight, white-knuckled fists at his sides, his tall, lean frame stiffening as a small, almost imperceptible flicker of fear crossed his sharp, angular features.

"Grace..." he said, his deep, gravelly voice low and shaky, his sharp, watchful eyes still locked onto the small, battered metal box in her trembling hands. "Where did you...?"

Grace felt her heart lurch, her mind spinning, her pulse thundering in her ears as she took another small, hesitant step forward, her trembling fingers clenching around the cold, rusted metal of the shovel handle as she forced herself to hold his sharp, watchful gaze.

"You buried them, didn't you?" she whispered, her voice low and trembling, her sharp, panicked breath echoing through the small, dimly lit hallway as she carefully set the small, battered metal box down on the small, wooden table by the door. "You buried them out in the garden... like some kind of... twisted secret."

David's sharp, watchful eyes flicked back up, locking onto hers for a brief, heart-stopping moment, his tall, lean frame still and silent, his sharp, calloused fingers clenching into tight, white-knuckled fists at his sides as a small, dark, almost predatory smile flickered at the corners of his mouth.

"And what if I did?" he whispered, his deep, gravelly voice low and menacing, his sharp, watchful eyes still locked onto hers as he took a small, predatory step forward, his tall, lean frame casting a long, jagged shadow across the small, dimly lit hallway.

Grace felt her breath catch in her throat, her heart racing, her mind spinning, her every nerve tingling with a dark, terrible anticipation as she stumbled back against the cold, hard wall, her trembling fingers clenching around the cold, rusted metal of the shovel handle as she forced herself to meet his sharp, watchful gaze.

"What else have you been hiding from me, David?" she

whispered, her voice low and trembling, her sharp, panicked breath echoing through the small, dimly lit hallway as she felt the cold, sharp knot of fear twist tighter and tighter in her stomach. "What else have you buried out there?"

David's sharp, watchful eyes flickered, his tall, lean frame still and silent, his sharp, calloused fingers clenching into tight, white-knuckled fists at his sides as a small, dark, almost predatory smile flickered at the corners of his mouth.

"That," he whispered, his deep, gravelly voice low and menacing, his sharp, watchful eyes still locked onto hers, "is something you'll have to find out for yourself."

The air in the small, dimly lit hallway felt thick and oppressive, the sharp, metallic clink of the old, battered shovel against the wooden floor echoing through the silent house like the slow, steady tolling of a funeral bell. Grace felt her pulse thundering in her ears, her breath coming in short, shallow gasps as she forced herself to hold David's sharp, piercing gaze, her trembling fingers still clenching around the cold, rusted metal of the shovel handle.

For a brief, heart-stopping moment, the world around her seemed to fade away, the sharp, suffocating silence pressing down on her from all sides, her every nerve tingling with a dark, terrible anticipation as she carefully stepped back, her sharp, panicked breath echoing through the small, dimly lit hallway.

David's sharp, watchful eyes flickered, his tall, lean frame still and silent, his sharp, calloused fingers clenching into tight, white-knuckled fists at his sides as a small, dark, almost predatory smile flickered at the corners of his mouth.

"Do you really want to know, Grace?" he whispered, his deep, gravelly voice low and menacing, his sharp, watchful eyes still locked onto hers as he took a small, predatory step forward, his tall, lean frame casting a long, jagged shadow across the small, dimly lit hallway. "Do you really want to know what I'm capable of?"

South London

A sharp, cold wind whipped through the narrow, rain-soaked

streets of South London, the dull, yellow glow of the flickering street lamps casting long, jagged shadows across the cracked, crumbling pavement as David stumbled down the narrow, deserted alley, his sharp, piercing eyes flicking back over his shoulder, his tall, lean frame hunched against the biting, freezing wind.

His sharp, calloused fingers were slick with blood, the dark, sticky liquid dripping down his trembling hands, splattering onto the cold, wet pavement below as he stumbled forward, his pulse thundering in his ears, his breath coming in short, sharp gasps as he forced himself to keep moving, his mind racing, his every nerve tingling with a dark, terrible anticipation.

He could still hear the sharp, muffled cries of the man he had left behind, the dark, gurgling sound of his shallow, ragged breathing echoing through the narrow, rain-soaked alley, the sharp, metallic clink of the blood-stained knife still ringing in his ears as he stumbled out onto the cold, deserted street.

David felt his breath catch in his throat, his sharp, piercing eyes flicking down to the dark, blood-stained blade clutched tightly in his trembling hand, his pulse thundering in his ears, his mind spinning, his every nerve tingling with a dark, terrible anticipation as he carefully wiped the blood from the blade, his sharp, calloused fingers still trembling as he carefully slipped the small, battered knife back into the deep, hidden pocket of his long, dark overcoat.

For a brief, heart-stopping moment, the world around him seemed to fade away, the sharp, suffocating silence pressing down on him from all sides, his every nerve tingling with a dark, terrible anticipation as he carefully ducked into the small, dimly lit doorway of a nearby building, his sharp, piercing eyes flicking back over his shoulder, his breath coming in short, shallow gasps as he carefully slipped inside, the sharp, metallic clink of the blood-stained knife still ringing in his ears.

He had been a different man then—sharp, reckless, dangerous. A man driven by dark, twisted desires, a man who thrived on the thrill of the hunt, the sharp, electric pulse of fear and anticipation that surged through his veins with every dark, terrible act.

But that had been years ago, a lifetime ago.

Or so he had thought.

Present Day

Grace felt her breath catch in her throat, her heart racing, her mind spinning, her every nerve tingling with a dark, terrible anticipation as she took another small, hesitant step back, her sharp, panicked breath echoing through the small, dimly lit hallway as she forced herself to hold David's sharp, watchful gaze.

"What... what have you done, David?" she whispered, her voice low and trembling, her sharp, panicked breath echoing through the small, dimly lit hallway as she felt the cold, sharp knot of fear twist tighter and tighter in her stomach. "What... what kind of man are you?"

David's sharp, watchful eyes flickered, his tall, lean frame still and silent, his sharp, calloused fingers clenching into tight, white-knuckled fists at his sides as a small, dark, almost predatory smile flickered at the corners of his mouth.

"The kind of man who doesn't make the same mistake twice," he whispered, his deep, gravelly voice low and menacing, his sharp, watchful eyes still locked onto hers as he took another small, predatory step forward, his tall, lean frame casting a long, jagged shadow across the small, dimly lit hallway.

Grace felt her breath catch in her throat, her heart racing, her mind spinning, her every nerve tingling with a dark, terrible anticipation as she stumbled back against the cold, hard wall, her trembling fingers clenching around the cold, rusted metal of the shovel handle as she forced herself to hold his sharp, watchful gaze.

"What... what do you mean?" she whispered, her voice low and trembling, her sharp, panicked breath echoing through the small, dimly lit hallway as she felt the cold, sharp knot of fear twist tighter and tighter in her stomach.

David's sharp, watchful eyes flickered, his tall, lean frame still and silent, his sharp, calloused fingers clenching into tight, white-knuckled fists at his sides as a small, dark, almost predatory smile flickered at the corners of his mouth.

"You're about to find out," he whispered, his deep, gravelly voice low and menacing, his sharp, watchful eyes still locked onto hers as he took another small, predatory step forward, his tall, lean frame casting a long, jagged shadow across the small, dimly lit hallway.

CHAPTER 10

The Watchful Eyes of Mrs. Whitmore

Grace leaned against the cool, chipped ceramic of the kitchen sink, her pulse still racing, her mind spinning, her every nerve tingling with a dark, terrible anticipation as she stared out through the small, rain-streaked kitchen window, her sharp, trembling fingers still clenched tightly around the cold, rusted metal of the old, battered shovel handle.

Outside, the long, tangled branches of the old oak tree swayed and creaked in the cold, biting wind, their long, jagged shadows flickering and dancing across the cracked, crumbling pavement below, their dark, twisted limbs casting long, ominous shadows across the small, dimly lit garden path.

Grace felt her breath catch in her throat, her sharp, piercing eyes flicking up to the small, darkened window of the old, crumbling house next door, her heart racing, her mind spinning, her every nerve tingling with a dark, terrible anticipation as she caught a brief, flickering glimpse of a small, shadowed figure peering out through the dark, rain-streaked glass.

Mrs. Whitmore.

The old woman had always been a quiet, unassuming presence in the small, close-knit neighborhood, her sharp, watchful eyes forever flicking out through the small, rain-streaked windows of her old, crumbling house, her long, bony fingers forever clutching at the tattered, yellowed lace curtains that hung like ghostly shrouds in the narrow, dimly lit windows.

Grace felt a small, sharp chill run down her spine, her sharp, trembling fingers still clenched tightly around the cold, rusted metal of the shovel handle as she carefully stepped back from the small, rain-streaked kitchen window, her sharp, piercing eyes still locked onto the small, darkened window of the old, crumbling house next door.

What had the old woman seen?

What did she know?

Two Weeks Earlier – Mrs. Whitmore's House

The small, dimly lit front room of the old, crumbling house was thick with the sharp, acrid smell of must and old, decaying wood, the long, jagged shadows of the tall, cracked wooden furniture flickering and dancing across the narrow, faded wallpapered walls as Mrs. Whitmore carefully eased herself down into the old, battered armchair by the narrow, rain-streaked window, her sharp, bony fingers still clutching tightly at the small, battered leather journal in her lap.

She felt a small, sharp chill run down her spine, her sharp, watery eyes flicking up to the small, rain-streaked window as she carefully reached up, her long, bony fingers trembling as she slowly pulled back the small, tattered lace curtain, her sharp, watery eyes flicking out through the narrow, rain-streaked glass, her breath catching in her throat as she caught a brief, flickering glimpse of the tall, lean figure moving quickly across the small, cracked garden path below.

David.

She felt her pulse quicken, her breath coming in short, shallow gasps as she carefully leaned forward, her sharp, watery eyes still locked onto the small, rain-streaked window, her sharp, bony fingers still clutching tightly at the small, battered leather journal in her lap as she carefully watched the tall, lean figure slip silently into the small, dimly lit back door of the old, crumbling house next door.

She had seen him come and go at odd hours, his tall, lean frame slipping in and out of the small, dimly lit back door, his sharp, watchful eyes forever flicking back over his shoulder, his every movement sharp, quick, and furtive, his sharp, calloused fingers forever clenching into tight, white-knuckled fists at his sides.

And then, just as quickly as he had appeared, he would be gone, his tall, lean frame slipping back out into the dark, rain-soaked garden, his sharp, watchful eyes forever flicking back over his shoulder as he carefully ducked back into the narrow, dimly lit alley that ran along the back of the old, crumbling house.

She felt her pulse quicken, her breath coming in short, shallow gasps as she carefully flipped open the small, battered leather journal in her lap, her long, bony fingers trembling as she quickly scribbled down the small, sharp notes in her sharp, tight, spidery handwriting, her sharp, watery eyes still locked onto the small, rain-streaked window as she carefully watched the small, dimly lit back door of the old, crumbling house next door.

Present Day—Grace's Kitchen

Grace felt her breath catch in her throat, her heart racing, her mind spinning, her every nerve tingling with a dark, terrible anticipation as she carefully set the old, battered shovel down against the chipped ceramic of the kitchen sink, her sharp, trembling fingers still clenched tightly around the cold, rusted metal handle as she carefully stepped back from the small, rain-streaked kitchen window, her sharp, piercing eyes still locked onto the small, darkened window of the old, crumbling house next door.

What had the old woman seen?

What did she know?

And what had she written down in that small, battered leather journal she always clutched so tightly in her long, bony fingers?

Grace felt a small, sharp chill run down her spine, her pulse racing, her mind spinning, her every nerve tingling with a dark, terrible anticipation as she carefully reached for her coat, her sharp, trembling fingers still clenching tightly around the cold, rusted metal of the shovel handle as she carefully slipped out the small, dimly lit back door, her sharp, piercing eyes still locked onto the small, darkened window of the old, crumbling house next door.

She needed to know.

She needed to know what the old woman had seen.

And she needed to know what the old woman had written down in that small, battered leather journal.

The air in the narrow alley behind Grace's house was thick with the sharp, acrid smell of wet earth and decaying leaves, the long, jagged shadows of the tall, cracked wooden fences flickering and dancing across the narrow, rain-soaked cobblestones as Grace carefully stepped out into the cold, biting wind, her sharp, trembling fingers still clutching tightly around the cold, rusted metal of the small, battered garden trowel she had grabbed from the small, dimly lit kitchen.

She felt her breath catch in her throat, her heart racing, her mind spinning, her every nerve tingling with a dark, terrible anticipation as she carefully slipped through the narrow, dimly lit garden gate that led to the small, cracked garden path behind Mrs. Whitmore's old, crumbling house.

The old woman's house loomed tall and dark in the cold, biting wind, its long, twisted, ivy-covered walls rising up like the jagged, crumbling bones of some ancient, forgotten creature, its long, shattered windows flickering and dancing with the sharp, jagged reflections of the cold, rain-soaked moonlight.

Grace felt a small, sharp chill run down her spine, her sharp, piercing eyes flicking up to the small, darkened window of the old, crumbling house as she carefully reached for the small, rusted metal door handle, her sharp, trembling fingers still clenched tightly around the cold, rusted metal of the small, battered garden trowel as she carefully eased the small, creaking back door open, her sharp, piercing eyes still locked onto the long, jagged shadows that flickered and danced across the narrow, rain-soaked floorboards of the old, crumbling hallway beyond.

The air inside the old, crumbling house was thick with the sharp, acrid smell of dust and old, decaying wood, the long, jagged shadows of the tall, cracked wooden furniture flickering and dancing across the narrow, faded wallpapered walls as Grace carefully stepped into the small, dimly lit front room, her sharp, trembling fingers still clenching tightly around the cold, rusted metal of the small, battered garden trowel as she carefully eased the small, creaking door shut behind her.

She felt her breath catch in her throat, her heart racing, her mind spinning, her every nerve tingling with a dark, terrible anticipation as she carefully stepped forward, her sharp, piercing eyes flicking up to the small, rain-streaked window at the far end of the narrow, dimly lit hallway, her sharp, trembling fingers still clenching tightly around the cold, rusted metal of the small, battered garden trowel as she carefully eased herself down into the small, battered armchair by the narrow, rain-streaked window.

There, on the small, cracked wooden side table beside the old, battered armchair, sat the small, battered leather journal she had seen the old woman clutching so tightly in her long, bony fingers.

Grace felt her pulse quicken, her breath coming in short, shallow gasps as she carefully reached for the small, battered leather journal, her sharp, trembling fingers still clenching tightly around the cold, rusted metal of the small, battered garden trowel as she carefully flipped open the small, battered leather cover, her sharp, piercing eyes flicking down to the small, tight, spidery handwriting that filled the narrow, yellowed pages.

The Journal's Secrets

February 14th – 3:47 AM The man with the sharp, watchful eyes slipped out the small, dimly lit back door again last night, his tall, lean frame slipping quickly through the narrow, rain-soaked alley, his sharp, calloused fingers forever clenching into tight, white-knuckled fists at his sides. He looked different this time, his sharp, piercing eyes flicking back over his shoulder, his every movement sharp, quick, and furtive, his long, dark coat flapping like a ghostly shroud in the cold, biting wind.

March 3rd – 2:12 AM I saw him again tonight, his tall, lean frame slipping quickly through the narrow, rain-soaked alley, his sharp, watchful eyes forever flicking back over his shoulder, his sharp, calloused fingers forever clenching into tight, white-knuckled fists at his sides. He looked different this time, his sharp, piercing eyes flicking back over his shoulder, his every movement sharp, quick, and furtive, his long, dark coat flapping like a ghostly shroud in the cold, biting wind. I swear, he saw me watching him this time.

April 22nd – 4:09 AM I know what he's hiding. I know what he's done. I know who he is.

Grace felt a small, sharp chill run down her spine, her pulse racing, her mind spinning, her every nerve tingling with a dark, terrible anticipation as she carefully flipped back to the small, tight, spidery handwriting at the front of the small, battered leather journal, her sharp, piercing eyes flicking down to the small, tight, spidery handwriting that filled the narrow, yellowed pages.

And there, scrawled in sharp, tight, spidery handwriting across the small, yellowed page, were the words that sent a cold, sharp chill running down Grace's spine:

"I know his secret."

Grace felt her breath catch in her throat, her sharp, trembling fingers still clenching tightly around the cold, rusted metal of the small, battered garden trowel as she carefully eased herself back from the small, cracked wooden side table, her sharp, piercing eyes still locked onto the small, battered leather journal that sat beside the old, battered armchair.

What did the old woman know?

What had she seen?

And how much danger was Grace really in?

CHAPTER 11

The Watcher in the Shadows

Grace's heart raced as she quickly slipped the small, battered leather journal back onto the cracked wooden side table, her sharp, trembling fingers still clenching tightly around the cold, rusted metal of the small, battered garden trowel as she carefully eased herself back from the narrow, rain-streaked window, her sharp, piercing eyes flicking nervously to the small, cracked wooden doorway that led back out into the narrow, dimly lit hallway.

Suddenly, the sharp, creaking sound of footsteps echoed through the narrow, rain-soaked hall, the long, jagged shadows flickering and dancing across the narrow, faded wallpapered walls as the old, creaking floorboards groaned and shuddered beneath the weight of the approaching figure.

Grace felt a small, sharp chill run down her spine, her pulse racing, her mind spinning, her every nerve tingling with a dark, terrible anticipation as the sharp, creaking sound of the approaching footsteps grew closer and closer, the long, jagged shadows flickering and dancing across the narrow, faded wallpapered walls as the old, cracked wooden door at the far end of the narrow hallway slowly creaked open, a long, thin sliver of sharp, cold moonlight spilling into the narrow, dimly lit front room.

"Grace."

The sharp, harsh whisper cut through the cold, biting silence like a jagged knife, the long, twisted shadows flickering and dancing across the narrow, rain-soaked floorboards as the tall, thin figure of Mrs. Whitmore slowly stepped into the small, dimly lit front room, her long, bony fingers still clenching tightly around the small, rusted metal handle of her old, battered walking cane as she carefully eased herself down into the small, battered armchair beside the narrow, rain-streaked window.

For a moment, the old woman said nothing, her sharp, piercing eyes flicking slowly up to meet Grace's, her thin, cracked lips twisting into a small, tight, knowing smile as she carefully leaned forward, her long, bony fingers still clenching tightly around the small, rusted metal handle of her old, battered walking cane as she carefully rested her long, bony elbows on the small, cracked wooden side table beside the narrow, rain-streaked window.

"I know why you're here," the old woman whispered, her sharp, piercing eyes still locked onto Grace's, her thin, cracked lips still twisted into that small, tight, knowing smile as she carefully leaned closer, her long, bony fingers still clenching tightly around the small, rusted metal handle of her old, battered walking cane.

Grace felt her pulse quicken, her breath coming in short, shallow gasps as she carefully leaned back in the small, battered armchair, her sharp, trembling fingers still clenching tightly around the cold, rusted metal of the small, battered garden trowel as she carefully met the old woman's sharp, piercing gaze.

"I know his secret," Mrs. Whitmore whispered, her sharp, piercing eyes still locked onto Grace's, her thin, cracked lips still twisted into that small, tight, knowing smile as she carefully leaned even closer, her long, bony fingers still clenching tightly around the small, rusted metal handle of her old, battered walking cane.

Grace felt a small, sharp chill run down her spine, her pulse racing, her mind spinning, her every nerve tingling with a dark, terrible anticipation as the old woman carefully leaned back in the small, battered armchair, her sharp, piercing eyes still locked onto Grace's, her thin, cracked lips still twisted into that small, tight, knowing smile.

"I know what he's hiding," the old woman whispered, her sharp, piercing eyes still locked onto Grace's, her thin, cracked lips still twisted into that small, tight, knowing smile as she carefully leaned even closer, her long, bony fingers still clenching tightly around the small, rusted metal handle of her old, battered walking cane.

"And I know who you are."

Grace felt her breath catch in her throat, her sharp, trembling fingers still clenching tightly around the cold, rusted metal of the small, battered garden trowel as she carefully leaned back in the small, battered armchair, her sharp, piercing eyes still locked onto the old woman's sharp, piercing gaze.

"What... what do you mean?" Grace stammered, her sharp, trembling fingers still clenching tightly around the cold, rusted metal of the small, battered garden trowel as she carefully leaned back in the small, battered armchair, her sharp, piercing eyes still locked onto the old woman's sharp, piercing gaze.

"I know what he's hiding," the old woman whispered, her sharp, piercing eyes still locked onto Grace's, her thin, cracked lips still twisted into that small, tight, knowing smile as she carefully leaned even closer, her long, bony fingers still clenching tightly around the small, rusted metal handle of her old, battered walking cane.

"I know what he did."

"And I know what you did."

The Past Comes Crashing Back

For a long, terrible moment, the small, dimly lit front room was filled with nothing but the sharp, harsh sound of Grace's shallow, ragged breathing, the long, jagged shadows flickering and dancing across the narrow, rain-soaked floorboards as the old woman carefully leaned back in the small, battered armchair, her sharp, piercing eyes still locked onto Grace's, her thin, cracked lips still twisted into that small, tight, knowing smile.

"You see, Grace," the old woman whispered, her sharp, piercing eyes still locked onto Grace's, her thin, cracked lips still twisted into that small, tight, knowing smile as she carefully leaned even closer, her long, bony fingers still clenching tightly around the small, rusted metal handle of her old, battered walking cane, "you're not the only one with secrets."

Grace felt a small, sharp chill run down her spine, her pulse racing, her mind spinning, her every nerve tingling with a dark, terrible anticipation as the old woman carefully leaned back in the small, battered armchair, her sharp, piercing eyes still locked onto Grace's, her thin, cracked lips still twisted into that small, tight, knowing smile.

"I know about the night in Melbourne."

Grace felt her breath catch in her throat, her sharp, trembling fingers still clenching tightly around the cold, rusted metal of the small, battered garden trowel as she carefully leaned back in the small, battered armchair, her sharp, piercing eyes still locked onto the old woman's sharp, piercing gaze.

"What... what do you mean?" Grace stammered, her sharp, trembling fingers still clenching tightly around the cold, rusted metal of the small, battered garden trowel as she carefully leaned back in the small, battered armchair, her sharp, piercing eyes still locked onto the old woman's sharp, piercing gaze.

"I know about the accident."

Grace felt a small, sharp chill run down her spine, her pulse racing, her mind spinning, her every nerve tingling with a dark, terrible anticipation as the old woman carefully leaned back in the small, battered armchair, her sharp, piercing eyes still locked onto Grace's, her thin, cracked lips still twisted into that small, tight, knowing smile.

The old woman's words hung heavily in the cold, damp air, the long, jagged shadows flickering and dancing across the narrow, rain-soaked floorboards as Grace carefully leaned back in the small, battered armchair, her sharp, trembling fingers still clenching tightly around the cold, rusted metal of the small, battered garden trowel.

For a long, terrible moment, the small, dimly lit front room was filled with nothing but the sharp, harsh sound of Grace's shallow, ragged breathing, her pulse racing, her mind spinning, her every nerve tingling with a dark, terrible anticipation as the old woman carefully leaned back in the small, battered armchair, her sharp, piercing eyes still locked onto Grace's, her thin, cracked lips still twisted into that small, tight, knowing smile.

"I know about the accident," Mrs. Whitmore whispered, her sharp, piercing eyes still locked onto Grace's, her thin, cracked lips still twisted into that small, tight, knowing smile as she carefully leaned even closer, her long, bony fingers still clenching tightly around the small, rusted metal handle of her old, battered walking cane.

Grace felt her breath catch in her throat, her sharp, trembling fingers still clenching tightly around the cold, rusted metal of the small, battered garden trowel as she carefully leaned back in the small, battered armchair, her sharp, piercing eyes still locked onto the old woman's sharp, piercing gaze.

"What... what accident?" Grace stammered, her pulse racing, her mind spinning, her every nerve tingling with a dark, terrible anticipation as the old woman carefully leaned back in the small, battered armchair, her sharp, piercing eyes still locked onto Grace's, her thin, cracked lips still twisted into that small, tight, knowing smile.

"The accident in Melbourne," Mrs. Whitmore whispered, her sharp, piercing eyes still locked onto Grace's, her thin, cracked lips still twisted into that small, tight, knowing smile as she carefully leaned even closer, her long, bony fingers still clenching tightly around the small, rusted metal handle of her old, battered walking cane.

"The one that changed everything."

For a long, terrible moment, the small, dimly lit front room was filled with nothing but the sharp, harsh sound of Grace's shallow, ragged breathing, the long, jagged shadows flickering and dancing across the narrow, rain-soaked floorboards as the old woman carefully leaned back in the small, battered armchair, her sharp, piercing eyes still locked onto Grace's, her thin, cracked lips still twisted into that small, tight, knowing smile.

"I was there that night," Mrs. Whitmore whispered, her sharp, piercing eyes still locked onto Grace's, her thin, cracked lips still twisted into that small, tight, knowing smile as she carefully leaned even closer, her long, bony fingers still clenching tightly around the small, rusted metal handle of her old, battered walking cane.

"I saw everything."

Grace felt a small, sharp chill run down her spine, her pulse racing, her mind spinning, her every nerve tingling with a dark, terrible anticipation as the old woman carefully leaned back in the small, battered armchair, her sharp, piercing eyes still locked onto Grace's, her thin, cracked lips still twisted into that small, tight, knowing smile.

"It was my son," Mrs. Whitmore whispered, her sharp, piercing eyes still locked onto Grace's, her thin, cracked lips still twisted into that small, tight, knowing smile as she carefully leaned even closer, her long, bony fingers still clenching tightly around the small, rusted metal handle of her old, battered walking cane. Grace felt her breath catch in her throat, her sharp, trembling fingers still clenching tightly around the cold, rusted metal of the small, battered garden trowel as she carefully leaned back in the small, battered armchair, her sharp, piercing eyes still locked onto the old woman's sharp, piercing gaze.

"Your husband was driving the car that killed my son."

Grace felt the small, sharp chill in her spine intensify, her pulse racing, her mind spinning, her every nerve tingling with a dark, terrible anticipation as the old woman carefully leaned back in the small, battered armchair, her sharp, piercing eyes still locked onto Grace's, her thin, cracked lips still twisted into that small, tight, knowing smile.

"And I have never forgotten."

Grace felt her breath catch in her throat, her sharp, trembling fingers still clenching tightly around the cold, rusted metal of the small, battered garden trowel as she carefully leaned back in the small, battered armchair, her sharp, piercing eyes still locked onto the old woman's sharp, piercing gaze.

"I've been watching him for years," Mrs. Whitmore whispered, her sharp, piercing eyes still locked onto Grace's, her thin, cracked lips still twisted into that small, tight, knowing smile as she carefully leaned even closer, her long, bony fingers still clenching tightly around the small, rusted metal handle of her old, battered walking cane.

"I know what he did."

"I know who he really is."

For a long, terrible moment, the small, dimly lit front room was filled with nothing but the sharp, harsh sound of Grace's shallow, ragged breathing, the long, jagged shadows flickering and dancing across the narrow, rain-soaked floorboards as the old woman carefully leaned back in the small, battered armchair, her sharp, piercing eyes still locked onto Grace's, her thin, cracked lips still twisted into that small, tight, knowing smile.

"I know everything."

Grace felt a small, sharp chill run down her spine, her pulse racing, her mind spinning, her every nerve tingling with a dark, terrible anticipation as the old woman carefully leaned back in the small, battered armchair, her sharp, piercing eyes still locked onto Grace's, her thin, cracked lips still twisted into that small, tight, knowing smile.

"And now you know too."

CHAPTER 12

The Puppet Master

The room seemed to shrink around Grace, suffocating her with the sheer weight of Mrs. Whitmore's revelation. Her heart pounded, each beat echoing the disbelief pulsing through her veins. David had been responsible for Mrs. Whitmore's son's death? How could she not have known?

Mrs. Whitmore's lips curled into a faint, almost triumphant smile as she watched Grace struggle to process the bombshell. She leaned back in her creaky armchair, the dim light of the single lamp casting eerie shadows over her deeply lined face.

"It wasn't just an accident," Mrs. Whitmore whispered. "Your husband was drunk. They didn't report that part in the news – they kept it quiet. But I knew. I was at the hospital when they brought my son in. I saw David, barely able to stand, his clothes stained with blood. He didn't even know what he had done. They covered it up because of his family connections."

Grace's mouth went dry. David had always said he hated Melbourne, that it held bad memories. She thought it was just the stress of his accident, his blindness. But now, the pieces were rearranging themselves into a dark, horrifying picture.

Mrs. Whitmore tapped her cane on the floor, her voice low and deliberate. "When I moved into this neighborhood, I recognized him immediately. His voice. The way he walked. A man can change his appearance, but his gait and his voice – they don't lie."

Grace stared at the old woman, stunned. "You moved here because of him?"

A sly smile flickered across Mrs. Whitmore's face. "I wanted to see what kind of life he had built after destroying mine. I needed to see if he suffered the way I did. But then... something changed."

Grace's brow furrowed. "What do you mean?"

"I saw how you cared for him. How you treated him like he was your whole world. And I realized, why should I hurt him when I could hurt you both?"

Grace felt a shiver crawl down her spine. "You've been tormenting me?"

The old woman chuckled softly. "All those little things? The garden tools that disappeared, the noise complaints, the whispers around the neighborhood – that was just the beginning. But then I discovered his secret. When he regained his sight and didn't tell you... I knew I had my ace. So, I fed you just enough to make you suspicious."

Grace's stomach churned as she remembered the strange notes in the mailbox, the cryptic messages on her phone. Mrs. Whitmore had been behind it all.

Mrs. Whitmore leaned forward, her eyes glinting with a twisted satisfaction. "I didn't just want him to feel guilt – I wanted his world to crumble. I wanted you to see him for what he truly is. A liar. A coward. A murderer."

A cold sweat broke out on Grace's forehead. "You've been manipulating me – trying to push me to confront him."

"Because that's the only way he'll feel true pain," Mrs. Whitmore hissed. "If you walk away from him, his perfect little life will collapse. That's what he deserves."

Grace couldn't believe what she was hearing. "You're... you're sick."

"Am I?" Mrs. Whitmore sneered. "Or am I just someone who refuses to let him get away with murder? You're just collateral damage."

Grace felt a wave of nausea rising within her. Mrs. Whitmore had embedded herself into their lives just to destroy them from the inside.

Suddenly, the sound of footsteps on the gravel path outside jolted them both. David's familiar silhouette appeared in the doorway, his face shadowed in the dim porch light.

"What's going on here?" he demanded, his eyes darting between the two women.

Mrs. Whitmore's mouth twisted into a smirk. "Ah, the man of the hour. Just in time."

David looked confused. "Grace, what are you doing here?"

Grace couldn't hold back any longer. "David, did you know? Did you know she's the mother of the boy from the accident?"

David's face went white, his jaw tightening. "What are you talking about?"

Mrs. Whitmore rose from her chair, pointing her cane at him. "You killed my son, David. And you thought you could run away from it."

David swallowed hard, his eyes flickering with guilt. "I didn't know... I didn't realize..."

Grace's voice shook with anger and betrayal. "David, did you really cause that accident?"

He didn't answer, his shoulders slumping under the weight of the truth. Mrs. Whitmore barked out a bitter laugh. "Coward. You've always been a coward."

Grace couldn't breathe, couldn't think. Everything she thought she knew about David was unraveling before her eyes. She wanted to scream at him, to demand why he'd kept such a devastating secret. But more than that, she wanted to know why he didn't tell her when he got his sight back.

Mrs. Whitmore stepped forward, whispering into Grace's ear. "Leave him. He doesn't deserve your loyalty. If you really loved yourself, you'd walk away."

David looked like a broken man, his hands trembling as he reached out to her. "Grace, I... I'm sorry."

But Grace pulled away, her heart pounding. She couldn't bear to look at him.

Mrs. Whitmore's parting words lingered in the air like a curse. "People like him don't change. They just learn to hide their sins better."

As Grace walked out into the cold, rainy night, she heard David's choked sob behind her. The illusion of her perfect marriage had been shattered. The man she thought she knew was a stranger, and the truth was a cold, bitter poison that seeped into her soul. As Grace sat in her car, hands gripping the wheel, a sense of dread washed over her. She wasn't just battling David's lies. She was caught in a twisted game orchestrated by a vengeful woman who had nothing left to lose.

But one question gnawed at her: If Mrs. Whitmore had known all along, why wait until now to reveal the truth? Was she telling the whole story, or was there another layer to her twisted plan? Grace needed answers – but first, she needed to confront the man who had broken her heart and shattered her trust.

Grace sat alone in the car, her fingers still trembling as they clutched the steering wheel. The rain pattered against the windshield, each drop a tiny, sharp reminder of the storm now raging inside her. She felt like a puppet, strings pulled by an unseen hand, manipulated by lies and half-truths.

David, the man she had loved and trusted, was no longer just her husband. He was a stranger. A liar. A killer.

She replayed Mrs. Whitmore's words in her mind, the venom in the old woman's voice echoing like a dark mantra. **"People like him don't change. They just learn to hide their sins better."**

When Grace finally returned home, the house felt different – colder, as if the walls themselves held their breath, sensing the cracks forming in her world. She dropped her keys on the hallway table, the clatter louder than usual in the oppressive silence. She hesitated at the foot of the stairs, her mind replaying every tender moment, every whispered promise, every shared dream.

David had already gone to bed, the faint glow of their bedroom lamp seeping under the door. She took a deep breath, steadying herself before pushing the door open.

David lay on his side, his back to her, his breathing slow and steady. For a moment, she wondered if he had somehow slipped back into the facade, pretending that nothing had changed, that he hadn't just been exposed as a murderer.

Grace stood in the doorway, staring at his silhouette, the urge to scream, to shake him, to demand answers bubbling up within her. But she held it in, choosing instead to slip into the bathroom, locking the door behind her.

She stared at her reflection, the harsh white light casting deep shadows under her eyes. She barely recognized the woman looking back – her face pale, eyes hollow, lips pressed into a thin, bitter line. How had it come to this? How had she become a prisoner in her own life?

Grace gripped the edge of the sink, her knuckles turning white. She had to know the whole truth, not just Mrs. Whitmore's twisted version. She needed to confront David, to force him to face his sins. But how?

As she brushed her teeth mechanically, her mind raced. She remembered the old filing cabinet in the basement, the one David had insisted on keeping locked. He had claimed it held old work files and tax documents – boring, mundane things she had never bothered to question.

But now, Grace's instincts screamed that it held more than just paperwork. Perhaps it held the secrets of his past, the truth behind the accident, the reason for his sudden blindness and even his miraculous recovery.

That night, Grace waited until David's breathing grew deep and rhythmic. She crept out of bed, tiptoeing down the hallway, every creak of the wooden floor sending a jolt of fear through her. She reached the basement door, the cool draft whispering against her skin as she descended the narrow steps.

The cabinet stood against the far wall, a gray metal sentinel in the darkness. Grace hesitated for a moment, her hand hovering over the lock. She had seen David punch in the code once, back when they had first moved in, but she had never committed it to memory.

Closing her eyes, she forced herself to remember. David had a habit of using significant dates – birthdays, anniversaries. She typed in their wedding date. The lock beeped and flashed red.

She tried David's birthday. Another failed attempt.

Then, almost as a desperate afterthought, she entered the date of the accident – the day Mrs. Whitmore's son died. The lock clicked open, the sound echoing in the basement like the crack of a gunshot.

Grace's heart raced as she pulled the cabinet door open, her fingers trembling as she reached inside. Files, old photographs, medical records, and handwritten notes lay in messy stacks, like the remnants of a life carefully hidden away.

She pulled out a thick, weathered folder, the front labeled **"Accident – 2018"** in David's neat handwriting. Her stomach twisted as she flipped it open. Newspaper clippings, police reports, hospital discharge papers – it was all there, every detail of the accident that had shattered Mrs. Whitmore's life.

But as she scanned the documents, something didn't add up. David's blood alcohol level was listed as zero. Witness statements described him as alert and sober at the scene, not the drunken wreck Mrs. Whitmore had described.

Grace's pulse quickened. Why would Mrs. Whitmore lie about something so easily disprovable? Was she simply consumed by grief, or was there something more sinister at play?

At the bottom of the pile, she found a small, leather-bound journal. She flipped it open, her eyes widening as she realized what it was – a personal diary, full of David's thoughts and fears in the months leading up to the accident.

As she read, her breath caught in her throat. David had written about being followed, about strange phone calls and anonymous threats. He had become paranoid, convinced that someone was out to get him.

"I see her everywhere. That old woman with the gray hair, always watching, always lurking. She knows something. I don't know what, but she knows. She's waiting for me to slip up."

Grace felt a chill run down her spine. Mrs. Whitmore had been in his life long before they ever moved to this quiet neighborhood. She had been stalking him, weaving herself into his world, long before Grace even entered the picture.

And then, scrawled in David's shaky handwriting, a single line that made her blood run cold:

"I think she wants me dead."

Grace's hands shook as she closed the journal, her mind reeling. Mrs. Whitmore hadn't just been a grieving mother seeking justice. She had been a puppet master, pulling the strings of their lives, slowly tightening the noose around David's neck.

She stumbled back, her pulse roaring in her ears. She had to confront David, but this time, she needed to be ready. She needed to know the whole truth – every twisted, tangled thread that bound their lives together.

CHAPTER 13

Into the Abyss

Grace clutched the leather-bound journal to her chest as she climbed the basement stairs, each creak under her feet echoing like a countdown to something catastrophic. She felt the weight of David's secrets pressing down on her, like a stone tied to her ankle, dragging her deeper into a dark, suffocating abyss.

When she reached the top, she paused, her breath coming in shallow, fearful gasps. She half expected David to be waiting for her in the hallway, his eyes boring into her, demanding to know what she had found. But the house remained eerily silent, save for the steady hum of the refrigerator in the kitchen.

She closed the basement door quietly, her fingers trembling as she slid the bolt into place.

Grace hurried back to the bedroom, carefully placing the journal beneath a loose floorboard in her closet. She couldn't confront David yet – not until she had the full picture. Mrs. Whitmore had clearly been stalking him for years, planting seeds of fear and paranoia, but why? And why lie about the accident?

As she slipped back under the covers beside her husband, she felt his warmth radiating off the mattress, a sharp contrast to the icy fear coursing through her veins. She lay awake, staring at the ceiling, her mind spinning with unanswered questions.

The next morning, Grace found herself standing at Mrs. Whitmore's front door, her heart thundering in her chest. She had tried to convince herself to leave it alone, to pack her bags and run, but something deep inside her demanded answers.

When the door creaked open, Mrs. Whitmore's eyes widened

slightly, surprise flickering across her wrinkled face. She quickly composed herself, leaning heavily on her cane as she stepped aside.

"Grace, my dear, what a surprise. Come in."

Grace stepped inside, the musty air of the old house clinging to her like a cold, wet blanket. She noticed the thin layer of dust on the furniture, the neglected stacks of old newspapers piled against the walls, the faint smell of mildew that seemed to seep from the very bones of the house.

Mrs. Whitmore shuffled into the living room, lowering herself into her armchair with a slow, deliberate motion, her eyes never leaving Grace.

"What brings you here?" the old woman asked, her voice dripping with mock sweetness.

Grace clenched her fists, her jaw tightening. She refused to be manipulated any longer. "You lied to me," she said, her voice sharper than she intended.

Mrs. Whitmore's thin, cracked lips curled into a sly smile. "Oh? About what, dear?"

"About the accident. About David being drunk. I found his medical records. His blood alcohol level was zero. He was sober that night."

For a fleeting moment, Mrs. Whitmore's eyes darkened, a flash of something almost like fear crossing her features. But it was gone as quickly as it came, replaced by a cold, calculating stare.

"Records can be falsified," she said, her tone icy. "You can't trust what you read."

Grace took a step closer, her pulse racing. "But you were at the hospital. You said you saw him, barely able to stand, his clothes stained with blood. Why would you lie about that?"

Mrs. Whitmore's fingers tightened around the handle of her cane, her knuckles turning white. For the first time, Grace saw the cracks in the old woman's steely facade.

"Why are you so determined to defend him?" Mrs. Whitmore spat, her eyes narrowing. "After all he's done? After all the lives he's destroyed?"

Grace felt a surge of anger rise within her, her fear dissolving into a fierce, protective rage. "Because I need the truth, not your twisted version of it. You've been manipulating me, playing me like a puppet. But I won't be your pawn anymore."

For a long moment, they stared at each other, the air between them crackling with unspoken tension. Then, slowly, Mrs. Whitmore leaned back in her chair, her lips curling into a bitter smile.

"You want the truth?" she whispered, her voice low and dangerous. "Fine. But be careful what you wish for, my dear. Sometimes the truth is far uglier than the lies."

Grace took a shaky breath, her heart pounding so loudly she feared it might burst. She turned on her heel, storming out of the house, her footsteps echoing down the creaky front steps.

As she reached the sidewalk, she heard Mrs. Whitmore's voice, cold and sharp, cutting through the morning air like a blade.

"Watch your back, Grace. If you keep digging, you might not like what you find."

Grace froze, the chill of those words settling deep in her bones. She didn't turn around, forcing herself to keep walking, her fists clenched at her sides.

Back at home, Grace locked herself in the bathroom, her hands shaking as she splashed cold water on her face. She felt like a cornered animal, trapped between a dangerous predator and the gnawing fear that the man she had shared her life with was a stranger – a liar and possibly a killer.

She needed to find out the full truth, no matter how dark or twisted it might be. She couldn't let Mrs. Whitmore scare her into silence.

As she straightened up, her reflection stared back at her, pale and determined, eyes blazing with a newfound resolve.

"**I will find the truth**," she whispered to herself, her fists clenching. "**And when I do, I'll make both of them pay.**"

Grace barely slept that night. Every creak of the house, every rustle of the wind outside her window, felt like a warning, a whisper that she was on borrowed time. She had crossed a line with Mrs. Whitmore, poking the bear that had been silently lurking in the shadows of her life.

The next morning, Grace found herself pacing the kitchen, her mind replaying Mrs. Whitmore's chilling words. *"Watch your back, Grace."* It echoed in her mind like a dark chant, fueling her paranoia.

She was so lost in thought that she almost jumped out of her skin when she heard David's voice behind her.

"Morning, honey," he said, his tone light, almost too cheerful. He leaned in for a kiss, but Grace turned her face, letting his lips brush against her cheek instead.

David frowned, pulling back slightly, his eyes narrowing. "Everything okay?"

Grace forced a tight smile, her heart racing. "Yeah, just... didn't sleep well."

David studied her for a moment, his gaze sharp and probing, as if he could sense the growing distance between them. Grace felt her pulse quicken, the fear that he might somehow read her mind, uncover her secrets, tightening like a noose around her throat.

Later that afternoon, Grace was in the bedroom, carefully pulling the loose floorboard where she had hidden the journal. She flipped through its pages, scanning the chaotic scrawl of David's thoughts. Some pages were filled with strange diagrams, dates circled and underlined, and cryptic notes that made her blood run cold.

As she leaned closer to decipher one particularly messy entry, she heard the creak of the hallway floorboards outside the bedroom. She froze, her breath catching in her throat.

Footsteps.

She quickly shoved the journal back under the floorboard, her fingers trembling as she slid it back into place. She barely had time to stand up and compose herself before the door swung open.

David stood there, his eyes sharp and unreadable, his gaze sweeping over the room.

"Hey," he said slowly, his tone carrying a hint of suspicion. "What are you doing in here?"

Grace forced a smile, trying to steady her racing heart. "Just... looking for my sweater. It's been chilly lately."

David's eyes lingered on the spot where she had just replaced the floorboard, his jaw tightening for a brief, terrifying second. Grace felt a fresh wave of panic surge through her.

Then, just as quickly as the tension had appeared, David's face relaxed into a gentle smile.

"Alright," he said, stepping into the room and pulling her into his arms. "Just checking. You've seemed a bit off lately."

Grace felt her body stiffen in his embrace, her mind racing as she tried to appear calm, normal, loving – all the things she felt slipping through her fingers.

As David pulled back and headed for the bathroom, Grace let out a shaky breath, her knees threatening to buckle. She had to be more careful. One mistake, one slip, and he would know.

Later that evening, as they sat down for dinner, David's phone buzzed on the kitchen counter. He glanced at it, his expression tightening for a brief moment before he reached for it.

Grace noticed the name on the screen – *Unknown Number.*

David quickly silenced the phone, slipping it into his pocket, but not before Grace caught a glimpse of the message preview:

"We need to talk. Urgent. Same place."

She felt her stomach churn, her hands gripping the edge of the table so tightly her knuckles turned white.

That night, when David finally fell asleep, Grace crept out of bed, her heart pounding as she reached for his phone on the nightstand. Her hands trembled as she swiped up to unlock it, but her heart sank when she saw the fingerprint lock.

She gently lifted his hand, pressing his thumb to the sensor, praying he wouldn't wake up. After a tense few seconds, the screen unlocked, and Grace quickly navigated to the message app.

The message from the unknown number was still there:

"We need to talk. Urgent. Same place. You can't keep hiding this

forever."

Grace felt a chill run down her spine. What was David hiding? And who was he meeting in secret?

Suddenly, David stirred beside her, mumbling something in his sleep. Grace quickly set the phone back on the nightstand, slipping under the covers and forcing herself to breathe slowly, evenly, as if she had been asleep all along.

As the darkness closed in around her, Grace felt the walls of her life closing in as well, her once safe and familiar world now a web of lies, deceit, and barely contained terror.

Grace felt the cold morning air bite at her cheeks as she stepped out onto the front porch. The world around her seemed to pulse with a sinister energy, every rustling leaf and distant birdcall tinged with a sense of impending doom. She pulled her jacket tighter around her, her eyes scanning the quiet street.

She had to know more.

Later that morning, Grace found herself at the small, cluttered library a few blocks from their house. She had avoided this place for years, ever since David's accident, preferring the comforting chaos of her kitchen or the warm light of their sunlit living room. But now, the shadows felt like allies, the dim corners and whispering pages giving her a sense of anonymity she desperately needed.

She logged into one of the dusty old desktop computers, her fingers trembling slightly as she typed in the name *Dr. Charles Wallace.* She hadn't forgotten the unsettling conversation she had overheard between David and the doctor. If anyone knew what was really going on, it was Dr. Wallace.

A few articles popped up – mostly academic papers, medical conference speeches, and a handful of obscure interviews. Then, something caught her eye – a small news clipping from over a decade ago:

"Respected Neurosurgeon's License Suspended Over Allegations of Unethical Practices."

Grace's heart skipped a beat. She clicked on the link, and the grainy image of a younger, sterner-looking Dr. Wallace appeared on the screen, his eyes cold and unflinching. The article described a scandal involving experimental surgeries, patients left in worse condition, and a mysterious out-of-court settlement that had allowed him to keep practicing.

As Grace read on, the pieces started to fit together. Dr. Wallace wasn't just a doctor with a questionable past – he was a man willing to take risks, to play with people's lives, to push the boundaries of ethics for the sake of his twisted ambition.

Grace was so lost in thought that she didn't notice the figure approaching her from behind.

"Digging up ghosts, are we?"

Grace's blood ran cold. She turned slowly, her heart thundering in her chest. Mrs. Whitmore stood there, her sharp eyes gleaming with a mixture of curiosity and menace.

"Mrs. Whitmore," Grace stammered, quickly closing the browser tab. "I... I didn't hear you come in."

The older woman gave a thin, knowing smile. "Oh, I'm sure you didn't. You've been quite the busy bee lately, haven't you?"

Grace forced a laugh, trying to hide the panic rising within her. "Just... researching. For a project."

Mrs. Whitmore leaned in closer, her breath warm against Grace's ear. "You should be careful, Grace. Sometimes, the past has sharp edges. You might cut yourself."

Grace's pulse raced as the older woman straightened up, her eyes locking onto Grace's with an intensity that sent a shiver down her spine.

"And, my dear," Mrs. Whitmore whispered, her voice like the rustle of dry leaves, "watch your back."

Before Grace could respond, Mrs. Whitmore turned on her heel and disappeared into the stacks, her sharp footsteps echoing off the polished wooden floors.

Grace stumbled out of the library a few minutes later, her mind spinning. Mrs. Whitmore's sudden appearance, her cryptic warning – it was too much. She needed to clear her head, to piece together the fragments of this twisted puzzle.

As she reached her car, she caught a glimpse of a black sedan parked across the street. It looked oddly familiar, the same car she had seen parked outside Dr. Wallace's clinic the day she had followed David there.

Grace's breath caught in her throat as the driver's side window slowly rolled down, revealing a man with dark sunglasses and a sharp, angular face. He gave her a slow, knowing nod before rolling the window back up and driving off, the engine purring like a predator slipping back into the shadows.

Grace leaned against her car, her hands shaking. She had stumbled into something far darker than she had ever imagined – a twisted web of lies, deceit, and silent threats that now felt like they were tightening around her throat.

Grace couldn't shake the image of that dark sedan, the faceless man with the predator's nod. She felt the walls closing in, the shadows in her life growing thicker and more menacing. This was no longer about a husband keeping secrets. It was a battle against an invisible force – one that watched her every move.

That evening, Grace sat alone in the living room, her fingers wrapped tightly around a steaming cup of chamomile tea. The house felt too quiet, the kind of silence that hummed with hidden whispers. She had spent hours flipping through old photo albums, desperately trying to recall anything about Mrs. Whitmore – anything that might explain the strange connection she felt to the woman.

She had almost convinced herself that she was being paranoid when the doorbell rang. Grace jumped, her heart leaping into her throat. She set the cup down with trembling hands and walked cautiously to the door, peering through the peephole.

It was Mrs. Whitmore.

Grace hesitated for a second, then opened the door. The old woman stood on her porch, wrapped in a thick, gray shawl that made her look like a ghost from another era. Her eyes, sharp as ever, glinted in the dim porch light.

"May I come in?" Mrs. Whitmore's voice was steady, almost too calm, as if she had been expecting this moment.

Grace stepped aside, her heart racing. The old woman moved

past her with surprising grace, her thin frame casting long, twisted shadows against the hallway walls.

They settled in the living room, Grace sinking into the armchair while Mrs. Whitmore chose the corner of the couch, her bony hands resting on her lap like the talons of a patient vulture.

"I figured it was time we had a little chat," Mrs. Whitmore began, her voice cutting through the silence like a blade. "You've been asking questions. Digging where you shouldn't. That's dangerous."

Grace forced herself to meet the woman's eyes, fighting the urge to shrink back. "What do you mean?"

Mrs. Whitmore's lips curled into a thin, humorless smile. "Oh, don't play coy, dear. I know you've been sniffing around. Dr. Wallace, your husband's little secret, the journal... You've stirred the pot."

Grace felt the blood drain from her face. How much did this woman know?

"Why are you here?" Grace managed, her voice barely above a whisper.

Mrs. Whitmore leaned forward, her eyes gleaming. "Because I've been where you are, Grace. I've loved a liar. I've lived in a house full of whispers and half-truths. And I've seen what happens when you let those lies fester."

Grace felt her pulse quicken. She wanted to scream, to push the old woman out of her house, to demand answers. But something in Mrs. Whitmore's voice – a hint of bitter, broken nostalgia – kept her rooted to her seat.

"What do you know about David?" Grace demanded, her hands gripping the arms of her chair.

Mrs. Whitmore chuckled, a dry, rasping sound. "I know more than you think, my dear. I knew him long before you did. I knew the man he was before he became the man you married."

Grace's breath caught in her throat. This revelation hit her like a slap to the face. "What... what are you talking about?"

The old woman's eyes flicked to the hallway, where the faint outline of a family portrait hung in the shadows. She nodded toward it.

"David has always been a man of secrets. He's always known how to hide his true self, to play the part of the devoted husband, the loving partner. But behind those eyes lies a darkness you cannot imagine."

Grace felt a chill crawl down her spine. She had sensed it, the cold, calculating side of her husband – the part of him that had kept his miraculous recovery a secret, that had lied to her every single day.

Mrs. Whitmore leaned back, her eyes never leaving Grace's. "Be careful, Grace. When a man like David starts to unravel, the threads can choke you too."

With that, Mrs. Whitmore stood, her shawl falling from her thin shoulders like a pair of tattered wings. She walked slowly to the door, her steps echoing through the silent house. She paused at the threshold, glancing back over her shoulder.

"You have a choice, my dear. Keep digging and risk it all, or walk away and pretend you never saw the darkness beneath the surface."

And then she was gone, the door clicking shut behind her, leaving Grace alone in the flickering light of the living room, her heart pounding in her chest.

Grace sat in the suffocating silence for what felt like hours, her mind a whirlwind of fear and confusion. Mrs. Whitmore's words echoed in her head, each syllable a fresh wound.

David had secrets. Dark secrets. And if she kept pulling at the loose threads, she might just unravel the life they had built together.

But something in her gut told her she couldn't stop now. She had to know the truth – whatever the cost.

Grace's heart pounded long after Mrs. Whitmore's footsteps faded down the path. The old woman's warning replayed in her mind, a bitter echo that refused to die down. She had to know the truth – all of it. David's web of lies was tightening around her, and she was done being the naive, trusting wife.

She had a choice to make: confront him directly, or continue peeling back the layers of deceit until she reached the core of his twisted reality. And tonight, she chose the latter.

That night, Grace lay in bed, the glow of the moon casting eerie shadows across the ceiling. David slept beside her, his chest rising and falling in steady, peaceful breaths. She watched him for a long moment, her mind replaying every detail of Mrs. Whitmore's cryptic visit.

She needed proof. Something tangible to break through the fog of lies.

Quietly, she slipped out of bed, careful not to disturb him. She tiptoed into the hallway, the old floorboards creaking softly beneath her feet. The air was thick, every sound amplified in the stillness of the house.

Grace made her way to the study, the small room David had claimed as his sanctuary. She had always respected his privacy, his need for space to work and think. But tonight, those boundaries felt like a cruel joke. She flicked on the desk lamp, its harsh white light cutting through the darkness, revealing the clutter of papers, books, and notebooks scattered across the desk.

She started rifling through the drawers, pulling out files, receipts, anything that might reveal a hint of his secret. Medical records, bank statements, old letters – each piece of paper a potential key to unlocking the truth.

As she dug deeper, she found a small, black notebook tucked beneath a stack of financial reports. The cover was worn, the corners frayed from frequent handling. Her pulse quickened. She flipped it open, her eyes scanning the neatly written lines in David's sharp, precise handwriting.

The Journal of a Deceiver

January 4 – I saw her today. Her eyes, like a specter from the past, caught me off guard. How did she find me? I thought this part of my life was buried.

February 14 – Grace suspects nothing. I've played the devoted husband for so long it's second nature. But the shadows are closing in. The past has a way of bleeding through the walls.

March 28 – Wallace called today. He's losing his nerve. The old fool has grown a conscience. I'll need to pay him a visit – remind him of the stakes.

Grace's breath hitched. Her fingers trembled as she flipped to the most recent entry.

April 15 – She's getting too close. I underestimated her. Whitmore's whispers have stirred her suspicions. I'll have to deal with this. But how? How do you silence someone you once loved?

The notebook slipped from Grace's fingers, thudding softly onto the desk. Her mind reeled, the room spinning around her. The man she had loved, trusted, built a life with – he was a stranger. A manipulator. A liar.

She staggered back, her hand clutching the edge of the desk for support. Her pulse roared in her ears, drowning out all rational thought. David had been plotting, scheming, all while pretending to be the perfect, loving husband.

And worse, he had been planning to silence her.

Grace backed out of the study, her feet moving on autopilot as she stumbled into the hallway. She bumped into a side table, sending a porcelain vase clattering to the floor. The noise shattered the silence, echoing like a gunshot through the house. From the bedroom, she heard the rustle of sheets, the soft creak of the mattress as David stirred.

"Grace?" his groggy voice called out, thick with sleep. "Everything okay?"

She froze, her heart pounding so loudly she thought he might hear it. She forced herself to take a deep breath, to steady her shaking hands.

"Yeah," she managed, her voice thin and strained. "Just... dropped something. Go back to sleep."

There was a long, agonizing pause. She held her breath, waiting to hear his footsteps, to see his shadow stretch into the hallway. But then, mercifully, the bed creaked again as he settled back down.

Grace stood there for a long time, her mind racing, her body trembling with a potent mix of fear and rage.

She needed a plan. She needed to find out what David was truly capable of – and, most importantly, how far he would go to protect his secrets.

The next morning, as the sun crept over the horizon, Grace made her way to the garden, the cool morning air a stark contrast to the storm raging inside her. She took out her phone, her fingers shaking as she scrolled through her contacts.

She hesitated for a moment before tapping on a name – Detective Marcus Hayes, an old family friend and one of the few people she still trusted.

The phone rang twice before his deep, gravelly voice answered.

"Grace? This is a surprise."

She swallowed hard, forcing herself to sound steady. "Marcus, I need your help. I think... I think David is hiding something. Something dangerous."

There was a pause on the other end, the line crackling faintly.

"Alright," Marcus said slowly. "I'll be there in an hour."

As she hung up, Grace took a deep breath, her mind already churning through the possibilities, the dangers. She had just crossed a line, and there was no turning back.

CHAPTER 15

The Mask Cracks

Grace barely slept that night. The weight of the notebook, of David's carefully crafted deception, hung over her like a storm cloud. She couldn't shake the feeling that every creak of the house, every whisper of wind through the garden, was David watching her, waiting for her next move.

She sat at the kitchen table the next morning, her coffee untouched, her eyes fixed on the small patch of garden visible through the window. The flowers swayed gently in the morning breeze, a sharp contrast to the chaos in her mind.

The front door creaked open, and her heart skipped a beat. Heavy footsteps clomped down the hall, and then Marcus stepped into the kitchen, his tall frame casting a long shadow across the tiled floor.

"Morning, Grace," he said, his eyes narrowing slightly as he took in her pale face and trembling hands. "What's going on?"

Grace gestured for him to sit, her voice a shaky whisper. "Marcus, I found something... something terrifying."

She pulled the black notebook from her purse and slid it across the table. Marcus picked it up, his thick, calloused fingers flipping through the pages. His jaw tightened as he read, his eyes growing darker with each entry.

After a few minutes, he looked up, his face a mask of concern. "Grace, this is... this is serious. If these entries are real, David's been hiding a hell of a lot more than just a secret. He's dangerous."

Grace nodded, her throat tight. "I don't even know this man anymore. I've been living with a stranger."

Marcus leaned forward, his deep-set eyes locked onto hers. "Grace, you need to be careful. If he's been planning this for as long as it seems, he won't take kindly to you digging into his past. We need to play this smart."

That evening, as the sun dipped below the horizon, casting long shadows through the house, Grace forced herself to act normal. She cooked dinner, set the table, and waited for David to come home.

When he finally walked through the door, his eyes scanned the room, his face betraying a flicker of unease as he noticed Marcus's faint boot prints on the kitchen floor.

"Hey, honey," Grace said, her voice deliberately bright. "How was your day?"

David hesitated for a fraction of a second, his eyes narrowing slightly. "Good. Just the usual grind. You?"

"Oh, nothing special. Just did some gardening, cleaned up a bit. You know, the usual."

For a moment, they locked eyes, the air between them thick with unspoken tension. Grace's heart raced, but she forced herself to hold his gaze, to maintain the facade of a loving, oblivious wife.

David moved closer, his footsteps slow and deliberate. He reached out, brushing a strand of hair from her face, his fingers lingering a little too long against her skin.

"You seem... tense," he said, his eyes searching hers for any hint of betrayal.

Grace forced a smile, hoping it didn't look as brittle as it felt. "Just tired, I guess. It's been a long week."

David's lips curled into a small, knowing smile. "Well, you should rest. You've earned it."

As he stepped back, his eyes lingered on her for a moment longer, his gaze sharp and calculating. Grace felt a cold shiver run down her spine as he turned away, his footsteps echoing down the hall.

That night, as they lay in bed, Grace felt the weight of David's presence beside her like a dark, suffocating fog. She stared at the ceiling, her mind racing, her heart pounding.

Had he suspected something? Did he know she had found the notebook?

Her mind drifted back to Marcus's warning – that David wouldn't take kindly to her prying. She had to be careful, to stay one step ahead.

The next morning, as David left for work, Grace watched him from the kitchen window. His shoulders were tense, his movements too controlled, too precise.

She picked up her phone, her fingers trembling as she dialed Marcus's number.

"He's onto me," she whispered as soon as he answered. "I can feel it."

There was a long, tense silence on the other end before Marcus's voice came back, calm but laced with concern.

"Then we need to move fast. I've pulled some records on Dr. Wallace – he's more involved in this than we thought. I'm coming over. We need to talk."

As she hung up, Grace felt a surge of fear mixed with determination. She was in deep now, caught in a dangerous dance with a man who had mastered the art of deception.

But she wasn't backing down. Not now. Not ever.

Grace watched the door close behind David, his footsteps echoing down the front steps. She felt the tension in her body slowly release as the sound of his car engine faded into the distance. She had a small window of time before he returned – just enough to make her next move.

She hurried to the kitchen, grabbed the notebook, and flipped to the most recent entries. David's handwriting, once so familiar and comforting, now looked sinister, like the scrawl of a madman. She skimmed through the pages, her eyes catching phrases like *"eliminate the threat"* and *"remove the problem before it grows."*

She shuddered. Was he talking about her? Or Marcus? Or someone else entirely?

The phone rang, breaking the eerie silence. She snatched it up, her pulse racing.

"Grace, it's me," Marcus's voice came through the line, deep and urgent. "I'm outside. Let me in."

Grace rushed to the door, her fingers fumbling with the lock. She pulled it open to reveal Marcus, his eyes sharp, his jaw set in a hard line.

"Come in, quickly," she whispered, glancing over his shoulder to check the street for any sign of David.

They moved to the kitchen, where Grace slammed the notebook onto the table. Marcus picked it up, his eyes narrowing as he flipped through the latest entries.

"This is getting darker, Grace," he said, his voice low and grave. "He's not just hiding his sight... he's planning something. Something dangerous."

Grace sank into a chair, her hands trembling. "I don't know what to do, Marcus. I feel like I'm living with a stranger, a... a monster."

Marcus leaned in, his face inches from hers. "We need to get ahead of this. I've been digging into Dr. Wallace's past, and it turns out he's not just David's eye surgeon. He has connections to a shady pharmaceutical company – one that's known for human experiments and cover-ups. If David's involved with them, this is bigger than we thought."

Grace's eyes widened, her mind reeling. "But... why? Why would David get involved with something like that?"

Marcus's jaw clenched. "I don't know yet, but I have a hunch it has something to do with the accident... and maybe more."

Suddenly, the sound of tires crunching on the gravel driveway outside froze them both. Grace's heart dropped. She peered through the kitchen window, her breath catching as David's car pulled up, his shadow moving behind the windshield.

"Marcus, hide!" she whispered frantically, shoving him toward the pantry door.

He slipped inside, pulling the door shut just as the front door creaked open.

David's footsteps echoed through the hallway, slow and deliberate, as if he could smell the fear in the air. Grace forced herself to remain calm, her heart thundering in her chest.

"Grace?" David called, his voice light but laced with a subtle edge. "I thought you said you'd be running some errands today."

Grace pasted a shaky smile onto her face as he entered the kitchen, his sharp blue eyes sweeping the room. "I was, but... I just felt like staying in. You know, organizing a bit."

David's eyes flicked to the slightly ajar pantry door, his head tilting slightly. He took a step closer, his polished leather shoes clicking against the tiles.

Grace's breath caught in her throat as he paused, his hand hovering near the door handle.

"Something wrong?" she asked, her voice a little too high, a little too forced.

David's head snapped back to her, his lips curling into a small, chilling smile. "No, nothing at all. Just... felt like something was off."

He held her gaze for a long, torturous moment before stepping back, his expression shifting into a mask of domestic calm. "I'm going to grab a shower. Maybe we can have dinner together later?"

Grace nodded stiffly, her fingers gripping the edge of the kitchen counter. "Of course."

He turned and walked out of the kitchen, his footsteps fading up the stairs.

As soon as she heard the bathroom door click shut, Grace lunged for the pantry, yanking the door open. Marcus stumbled out, his face pale, his chest heaving.

"That was too close," he whispered, sweat glistening on his forehead.

Grace closed the pantry door behind him, her heart still racing. "We need to figure this out, Marcus. Before it's too late."

The Thin Line Between Love and Fear

That night, as David lay beside her, his breathing deep and steady, Grace stared at the ceiling, her mind a whirlwind of fear and suspicion. She could feel the darkness growing between them, like a shadow slowly swallowing their once-bright marriage.

But she was no longer the naive wife, the unsuspecting partner. She was on to him now, and no matter how dangerous this game became, she would not back down.

David might be the hunter, but she was no longer his prey.

Grace lay awake that night, her mind replaying the tense moments in the kitchen. David had been inches from discovering Marcus, and she knew it. The man she once trusted with her life now felt like a stranger, a dangerous one at that. She couldn't keep living like this – always on edge, always looking over her shoulder.

As David's breathing evened out beside her, slipping into the deep, dreamless sleep of a man without a guilty conscience, Grace's resolve hardened. She had to find proof, something undeniable, something that could strip away the charming mask David had carefully constructed.

She slowly slipped out of bed, her bare feet sinking into the cool carpet. Moving silently, she padded toward the hallway, avoiding the creaky floorboard near the door. She paused at the bedroom threshold, casting a final glance at David's motionless form before slipping out.

The house was eerily silent, the only sound the faint hum of the refrigerator in the kitchen below. Grace's pulse quickened as she approached the attic door at the end of the hallway. She had avoided this part of the house for years, ever since David's accident. It had become his sanctuary, his place of retreat when the world felt too harsh and unyielding.

Her hand trembled as she reached for the cold brass doorknob. It resisted at first, as if the attic itself sensed her intrusion. She twisted harder, and the door creaked open, a stale gust of trapped air brushing against her face.

A narrow, creaky staircase led up into darkness. Grace hesitated, her mind racing with images of what she might find – strange blueprints, weapons, or even a list of names scribbled in David's manic handwriting.

She took a deep breath, reminding herself why she was doing this. She needed to know the truth, no matter how ugly it was.

As she reached the attic, her phone's flashlight cut through the thick shadows, revealing forgotten boxes, old furniture, and dusty tarps. The air was heavy, tinged with the smell of aged wood and forgotten memories.

She moved carefully, stepping over piles of books and stacks of old newspapers. Then, in the corner, hidden behind a stack of paint cans and old sports equipment, she saw it – a small, metallic safe bolted to the floor.

Her heart pounded. She knelt beside it, brushing away a thick layer of dust. It was locked, of course, but a small keypad glowed faintly in the darkness. She hesitated, fingers hovering over the numbers. David wasn't the type to use his birthday or anything obvious, but he had a strange attachment to certain dates – the day they met, the day he regained his sight...

She tried a few combinations, her fingers shaking with each failed attempt. Then, a thought struck her – the day of his accident. It was the day their lives had changed forever. She punched in the numbers: 06212021.

The safe beeped, a single green light flickering on. It clicked open with a soft metallic clunk, and Grace's breath caught in her throat.

Inside, she found a stack of manila folders, a small black journal, and a sleek, silver flash drive. She grabbed them quickly, her fingers trembling as she flipped through the first folder. It contained medical records – not just his, but dozens of patients, each one with notes scribbled in David's precise handwriting.

The next folder was worse – photos, surveillance images of her, Marcus, even Mrs. Whitmore. Her heart raced as she saw a grainy image of Marcus entering their house just days ago.

But it was the journal that truly chilled her. It was filled with page after page of calculations, chemical formulas, and chilling notes like *"Test 3 – Subject responded positively to the serum. Full recovery expected within weeks."*

What the hell had David gotten himself into?

She snatched up the flash drive, her mind spinning. She needed to get this to Marcus, but the floorboards creaked behind her, and she froze.

"Grace?"

David's voice cut through the darkness like a blade. She spun around, her flashlight catching his face as he stepped into the attic, his eyes sharp and alert.

"What are you doing up here?" he asked, his tone dangerously calm.

Grace clutched the journal to her chest, her pulse thundering in her ears. She forced a tight, nervous smile. "I... I couldn't sleep. I thought I'd clean up a bit, you know, get rid of some old junk."

David's gaze dropped to the open safe, his jaw tightening for a fraction of a second before his lips twisted into a smile. He stepped closer, his shadow stretching across the attic floor like a dark omen.

"Funny," he said, his voice low and threatening. "I thought I locked that."

Grace took a step back, her mind racing. She had to get past him, had to get out of this attic before he realized what she had just found.

"Maybe you just forgot," she whispered, edging toward the staircase.

David's smile didn't reach his eyes as he took another step forward, closing the distance. "Maybe."

Before he could react, Grace spun around, sprinting down the stairs, her bare feet barely touching the steps. She heard David curse behind her, his heavy footsteps shaking the wooden planks as he lunged after her.

She hit the hallway, slamming the attic door shut behind her. She heard him crash into it, the doorknob rattling violently as he twisted it, roaring her name.

She didn't stop. She flew down the stairs, her heart hammering against her ribs, her hand still clutching the journal and flash drive. She burst through the front door, the cool night air hitting her like a slap to the face.

Grace stumbled onto the lawn, her mind screaming at her to keep moving, to run, to survive.

CHAPTER 16

Running in the Dark

The night air hit Grace like a cold slap to the face, shocking her back into the present. Her heart pounded against her ribs as she sprinted across the dew-soaked lawn, her bare feet sinking into the cold, damp grass. The journal and flash drive felt like burning coals in her hands, their weight a reminder of the dark secrets she had uncovered.

Behind her, the attic door crashed open. David's voice cut through the night, sharp and dangerous.

"Grace! Get back here!"

She didn't look back, refusing to give him the satisfaction of seeing her fear. She darted past the hydrangea bushes and into the side alley, the dim streetlights casting long, twisted shadows that seemed to reach for her as she ran.

She had no plan, no destination – just the primal urge to survive. The quiet suburban street felt like a labyrinth, each corner a potential trap. She turned sharply onto Birch Lane, her pulse thundering in her ears, drowning out the distant hum of car engines and the rustle of leaves in the wind.

Marcus' Apartment

Her mind latched onto a single thought – Marcus. He was the only one who might believe her, the only one she could trust now. She dug her phone out of her pocket, her trembling fingers struggling to find his number.

The line rang, each second stretching into an eternity. She glanced over her shoulder, half expecting David to come tearing around the corner, his eyes blazing with the fury of a man betrayed.

Finally, Marcus' groggy voice crackled through the speaker.

"Grace? It's almost midnight, what's –"

"Marcus, I need you," she gasped, her voice breaking. "I'm coming to your place. Just... just be ready."

"Wait, Grace, what happened? Are you okay?" His voice sharpened with concern.

"Just – I'll explain when I get there. Please."

She ended the call before he could press further, tucking the phone into her waistband as she ducked into a narrow side street.

The cold air burned her lungs, each breath a painful reminder of her panic. She skidded around a corner, narrowly avoiding a parked car, and cut through a small playground. The rusty swings clanged softly in the breeze, the creaking sound adding a twisted soundtrack to her desperate escape.

Then she heard it – the steady, measured footsteps behind her. David.

He had followed her, his heavier frame cutting through the darkness with a relentless, predatory stride.

"Grace," his voice echoed off the brick walls of the narrow alley. "You're making this harder than it needs to be."

She choked back a sob, her mind racing. She needed to lose him, to buy herself time. She ducked behind a row of garbage bins, her back pressed against the cold, damp wall of a convenience store. She forced her breathing to slow, her chest heaving with suppressed terror.

David's footsteps slowed, his shadow stretching across the cracked pavement as he scanned the darkness. She watched, her pulse a wild drumbeat in her ears, as he stepped into the flickering light of a streetlamp, his head turning slowly as he searched for her.

"I know you're scared," he called out, his voice disturbingly calm. "But I'm not the enemy here, Grace. You have to understand – this is all for us."

She tightened her grip on the journal, her mind flashing back to the disturbing notes and medical records she had found.

"Test 3 – Subject responded positively..."

What the hell had he been doing?

David's shadow loomed closer, his steps slow and deliberate, a hunter savoring the chase.

The Escape Route

Grace spotted a narrow gap between the convenience store and the adjacent laundromat, a dark, trash-strewn passage barely wide enough for her to slip through. She took a deep breath, steeling herself, and darted into the shadows, her heart pounding as the icy brick scraped against her shoulders.

She squeezed through, ignoring the sharp sting of broken glass underfoot, and stumbled out into a small back alley. She hesitated for a moment, then bolted down the uneven path, her eyes scanning for an exit.

Behind her, she heard David curse – a low, frustrated growl that sent a fresh wave of terror crashing over her.

She reached the end of the alley and burst onto a main road, the bright headlights of an oncoming car momentarily blinding her. She threw up her hand to shield her eyes, her legs nearly giving out as she staggered into the crosswalk.

The car screeched to a halt, the driver's panicked face illuminated by the harsh glow of the dashboard lights.

"Watch it, lady!" the driver shouted, leaning on his horn as Grace stumbled past, her mind too frenzied to form a coherent apology.

Marcus' building loomed ahead, a squat, brick structure with narrow windows and a flickering neon sign that read *Harrison Apartments.* She sprinted up the steps, slamming her fist against the buzzer for his apartment.

"Come on, come on, come on..." she whispered, her gaze flicking over her shoulder.

The door clicked open just as she caught a glimpse of a tall, dark figure rounding the corner, his shadow stretching ominously across the wet pavement.

She slipped inside, slamming the door behind her and leaning against it, her chest heaving as she struggled to catch her breath.

Marcus appeared at the top of the stairs, his eyes wide with concern as he took in her disheveled state.

"Grace, what the hell happened?"

She forced herself to meet his gaze, the journal and flash drive clutched tightly in her shaking hands.

"David... he's not who we think he is," she whispered, her voice a ragged, terrified rasp.

Marcus' eyes darkened, his jaw tightening as he stepped forward, his fists clenching at his sides.

"Then let's find out who he really is," he said, his voice low and determined.

Marcus led Grace up the creaking stairs, his apartment a few flights up. The narrow hallway felt like a tunnel, the flickering overhead lights casting jittery shadows that only added to her mounting dread. She clutched the journal and flash drive like lifelines, her breaths coming in short, panicked bursts as they reached his door.

"Get in," Marcus said, pushing the door open and quickly locking it behind them.

Grace sank onto the worn leather couch, her head spinning. The room was small and cluttered, a testament to Marcus' chaotic lifestyle – half-empty coffee cups, scattered newspapers, and a guitar propped against the corner wall.

Marcus grabbed a water bottle from the small kitchen and handed it to her, his eyes never leaving her face.

"Talk to me, Grace. What the hell is going on?"

She took a long sip, the cool water soothing her parched throat as she tried to gather her thoughts.

"David," she managed to croak. "He's... he's been lying to me. To everyone."

Marcus sat down across from her, leaning forward with his elbows on his knees, his dark eyes sharp and focused.

"What kind of lies? Is this about his eyesight? I knew something was off with him."

Grace shook her head, her fingers trembling as she placed the journal and flash drive on the coffee table.

"It's so much worse than that," she whispered. "He's been conducting experiments – secret, twisted experiments. I found his notes, his patient files... and it's not just about his sight. He's been using people, testing on them."

Marcus' jaw tightened, his fists clenching. "Testing what? What the hell are you talking about?"

She hesitated, the horrific images from David's journal flashing through her mind – the diagrams, the patient photographs, the cold, clinical descriptions of human suffering.

"He's been experimenting with some kind of neurological manipulation," she whispered. "Mind control, memory alteration... it's insane."

Marcus leaned back, his face a mixture of shock and disbelief.

"Mind control? Are you serious?"

She nodded, pushing the journal toward him. "Look for yourself. It's all in there – notes, diagrams, recordings. He's been testing this stuff on real people, Marcus. And I think... I think he's been using me."

Marcus picked up the journal, flipping through the pages with a growing sense of dread. He paused on a page filled with hastily scrawled notes and scratched-out lines, his brow furrowing as he read:

"Subject G – increased compliance observed... heightened emotional response... successful implantation of false memories..."

"Subject G?" Marcus muttered. "Grace, this... this can't be real."

She wrapped her arms around herself, feeling suddenly exposed. "I think I'm 'Subject G,' Marcus. He's been testing on me this whole time, manipulating my thoughts, my memories. That's why I've been feeling so out of control, why I can't remember certain things. He's been using me as a guinea pig."

Marcus' eyes darkened, a dangerous edge creeping into his voice. "That son of a b****. We need to take this to the police. This is criminal, Grace. He's crossed every line."

Grace shook her head, panic tightening her chest.

"No, not yet. If we go to the police now, he'll see it coming. He has connections, Marcus. You know how manipulative he can be.

We need to find out how deep this goes, how many people he's dragged into this."

Marcus set the journal down, his mind racing.

"Wait," he said slowly, his eyes locking onto hers. "You said this has been going on for a while, right? Since before his accident?"

Grace nodded, confused.

"What if he's not working alone?" Marcus continued, his voice dropping to a harsh whisper. "What if there are others involved – people who know about this, maybe even helping him cover his tracks?"

A cold chill ran down Grace's spine. The thought had crossed her mind, but hearing it spoken aloud made it all too real.

"You mean like a... a network?"

Marcus leaned in, his eyes intense.

"Exactly. If David is testing on people, manipulating memories, there's no way he's doing this alone. We need to find out who else is involved."

Grace's mind raced, the pieces of the puzzle clicking into place. Mrs. Whitmore – the nosy neighbor with her constant prying and uncanny ability to appear at just the right moment. Could she be part of this twisted web?

"What if Mrs. Whitmore knows something?" Grace whispered, her heart pounding. "She's always lurking around, always watching. What if she's more than just a nosy old lady?"

Marcus' eyes narrowed, his jaw tightening.

"Then we need to pay her a visit," he said, his voice grim. "But first, we crack this flash drive. If there's any proof of what David's been doing, it's in there."

He grabbed his laptop from the side table, powering it on with a determined click.

"Let's expose this bastard."

Marcus's fingers moved quickly over the keyboard, his eyes narrowed in concentration as the laptop hummed to life. The dim light from the screen cast long shadows on his face, highlighting the tension etched into his features. Grace sat beside him, her pulse racing as the flash drive clicked into the port.

"Alright," Marcus muttered, his eyes darting across the screen. "Let's see what David's been hiding."

Grace leaned in, her breath shallow, the cold realization of her husband's twisted double life settling into her bones. She clutched her knees, bracing herself for whatever secrets the drive might hold.

The first folder opened, revealing dozens of subfolders, each labeled with a code. Marcus scrolled through them, his jaw tightening as he recognized the cold, clinical language – *Subject A1, Subject G, Subject Z3...*

"Jesus, Grace," he whispered, glancing at her. "There are dozens of them."

She bit her lip, her stomach twisting.

"Open mine," she whispered. "Subject G."

Marcus hesitated for a moment before double-clicking the folder. It opened to reveal a collection of video files, audio recordings, and documents. He selected the first video file, the screen flickering for a moment before a grainy image filled the screen.

It was their living room. Grace's heart nearly stopped as she recognized the scene – herself, sitting on the couch, staring blankly at the wall, her head tilted slightly to the side as if in a trance.

"Grace," Marcus said, his voice trembling. "What the hell is this?"

The video played on, David's voice crackling through the laptop speakers.

"Day 42 – Subject G. Emotional response to the second memory implant has been positive. Subject remains unaware of the manipulation, demonstrating increased compliance and reduced independent thought. Progress is promising."

Grace slapped a hand over her mouth, the bile rising in her throat. She had no memory of this – of sitting like that, of being a puppet in her own home.

"Oh my God," she whispered, tears streaming down her face. "He's been... controlling me."

Marcus quickly clicked out of the video, his face pale.

"That's not just unethical, it's monstrous," he muttered, his fists trembling. "We have to take this to the police."

"Wait," Grace whispered, her eyes locking onto another file in the folder. "What's that?"

Marcus hesitated, the cursor hovering over a file titled *Project Obsidian – Command Protocols*. He clicked it open, revealing a series of complex codes, psychological triggers, and phrases meant to override a person's free will.

"Command Sequence Alpha – Subject G: Trigger phrase – 'Always Remember'... Expected Response – Full compliance without hesitation."

The words hit Grace like a physical blow. She remembered David whispering that phrase to her so many times – in the morning before work, late at night when she felt overwhelmed. It had always felt like a loving reminder, a comforting touch. But now, the truth twisted it into something sick and perverse.

Marcus leaned back, his eyes wide.

"Grace... this is... he's been brainwashing you."

Grace's hands trembled as she covered her mouth, her entire world collapsing around her. She felt the walls closing in, the air thinning.

"I need to get out of here," she whispered, standing abruptly. "I need to confront him."

"Grace, wait," Marcus said, grabbing her wrist. "If he's this dangerous, you can't just walk in there. We need a plan."

She pulled her arm free, her eyes blazing.

"I've been a prisoner in my own mind, Marcus. He's turned me into a puppet. I'm not hiding anymore."

Marcus hesitated, torn between his fear for her safety and his desire to see David brought down.

"Alright," he said, grabbing his car keys. "But you're not doing this alone. Let's end this."

As they stormed out of the apartment, the screen of the laptop blinked back to the main folder. For a brief moment, another file flashed into view – one they had missed.

"Subject W – Whitmore"
But they were already gone, the door slamming shut behind them as they sped into the night, ready to confront the monster David had become.

CHAPTER 17

The Trap

The night air was thick and suffocating as Grace and Marcus sped through the darkened streets. The city lights streaked past them like ghosts, silent witnesses to the chaos unfolding in Grace's mind. She clutched the seatbelt, her knuckles white, her pulse pounding in her ears.

"He's at the clinic," Marcus said, his voice tense. "I tracked his phone."

Grace's jaw clenched. She felt a surge of anger rise in her chest, hot and consuming, pushing aside the fear that had gripped her for so long.

"I want to look him in the eyes when I confront him," she whispered. "I need to hear him admit it."

Marcus glanced at her, his face shadowed in the flickering lights of passing street lamps.

"Are you sure you're ready for this?"

Grace's eyes narrowed, her lips pressing into a thin line.

"I've been a pawn in his twisted game for too long. It's time to flip the board."

They pulled up to the clinic, its sleek, glass facade reflecting the dim streetlights. It was a place that had once felt sterile and comforting, a symbol of David's dedication to his patients. Now, it felt more like the lair of a predator.

They stepped out of the car, their footsteps echoing on the polished tiles as they approached the entrance. Marcus reached for the handle, but Grace stopped him, her hand trembling slightly.

"Wait," she whispered, her eyes flicking to the security camera above the door. "He might be watching us."

Marcus hesitated, then nodded. He pulled a small, black box from his jacket – a signal jammer. He switched it on, and the tiny LED on the side blinked to life, cutting off any live feeds David might be monitoring.

They slipped inside, the darkness of the empty clinic swallowing them whole. The sharp, antiseptic smell clung to the air, mixing with the stale scent of fear that clung to Grace's skin.

They crept down the hallway, their breaths shallow, each step a calculated risk. Grace's mind raced, fragments of David's twisted recordings echoing in her thoughts.

"Command Sequence Alpha... Full compliance without hesitation..."

They reached David's private office – a heavy, steel door at the end of the hall, slightly ajar. Light spilled through the crack, casting a harsh line across the sterile white floor.

Marcus leaned in, pressing his ear to the door, then glanced back at Grace, his eyes filled with concern. He pushed the door open slowly, revealing David, his back to them, hunched over a bank of monitors. The screens flickered with live feeds from various rooms in the clinic, each one filled with sleeping patients, their heads wired with electrodes.

Grace's heart lurched as she realized she recognized some of the faces – neighbors, friends, even her own hairdresser.

David straightened suddenly, his head tilting slightly as if he sensed their presence. He turned slowly, his expression unreadable, a slight smirk playing at the corners of his lips.

"Grace," he said, his voice calm, almost pleased. "And Marcus. How... unexpected."

Grace stepped forward, her fists clenched at her sides.

"Unexpected?" she spat, her voice trembling. "You've been controlling me, manipulating my mind, twisting my thoughts... How could you?"

David's smirk widened, his eyes glinting with a dark, unhinged amusement.

"I did it for us, Grace," he said, his voice dripping with condescension. "For our marriage. For your own good."

Grace felt her knees weaken, her head spinning with the audacity of his words.

"For our good?" she choked out. "You turned me into a puppet, David! You stole my free will!"

David stepped around the desk, his gaze never leaving hers.

"Free will?" he echoed, his tone mocking. "Grace, free will is an illusion. Everyone is controlled by something – fear, desire, trauma. I just made it more... efficient."

Grace took a shaky step back, her mind reeling.

"You're insane," she whispered, her breath coming in short, panicked bursts. "You're a monster."

David's smirk twisted into a snarl, his calm facade cracking for the first time.

"And you're ungrateful," he snapped, his eyes blazing. "I gave you peace. I silenced your doubts, your fears, your self-destructive tendencies. I perfected you."

Marcus stepped forward, his fists balled.

"You're done, David," he growled. "We have everything – the files, the videos, the command protocols. You're going to rot in a cell."

David's eyes flicked to Marcus, a dangerous glint sparking in their depths.

"Oh, Marcus," he said, his voice dripping with disdain. "You have no idea how deep this goes."

Before they could react, David reached into his pocket, pulling out a small remote. He pressed a button, and the screens behind him flickered to black, then filled with a live feed of Grace's home – their living room, the front porch, even their bedroom.

Grace's blood ran cold.

"You see, Grace," David said, his voice dropping to a sinister whisper. "I've always been one step ahead."

The screens shifted, showing a figure stepping into Grace's home – a man dressed in black, his face obscured by a hood. He moved swiftly, silently, heading towards their daughter's room.

"No!" Grace screamed, lunging for David. "What have you done?"

David caught her wrists, his grip bruising, his face inches from hers.

"I told you, Grace," he hissed, his eyes blazing with twisted triumph. "I control everything."

Marcus lunged, ripping Grace from David's grasp and slamming him into the desk. The remote clattered to the floor, its buttons flickering red.

"You're not getting away with this," Marcus growled, his face inches from David's. "Not this time."

David's laugh echoed off the sterile walls, a dark, twisted sound that sent chills down Grace's spine.

"I already have," he whispered, his eyes dancing with madness. "I always do."

Grace's pulse raced as she stumbled back, her eyes locked on the live feed of their home. The shadowy figure crept closer to her daughter's bedroom, every step sending fresh waves of terror through her veins. She grabbed the remote from the floor, frantically pressing buttons, but the screens remained locked on the terrifying scene unfolding in her home.

Marcus twisted David's arm behind his back, slamming him against the desk.

"Call him off!" Marcus snarled, his teeth bared, every muscle in his body coiled with fury. "Tell him to stand down, or I swear I'll —"

David's twisted smile never wavered.

"Or you'll what?" he spat, his head snapping back to meet Marcus's gaze. "You don't have the guts, Marcus. You never did."

Grace felt the cold edge of panic clawing at her throat. She grabbed the phone from her pocket, her fingers trembling as she dialed the police.

"Please," she whispered, her voice cracking. "I need help. My daughter – someone's in my house. Please, hurry!"

She hung up, her hands shaking as she turned back to David.

"You monster," she whispered, her eyes brimming with tears. "How could you do this to us? To her?"

David's eyes gleamed with a dangerous light, his lips pulling into a mocking grin.

"Because, my dear," he said, his voice dripping with arrogance, "you never understood the lengths I'd go to for control."

Before she could respond, a soft chime echoed through the office – the sound of the clinic's main entrance sliding open. Grace's heart skipped a beat, fear twisting into a sharp, icy blade in her chest.

Marcus tightened his grip on David's arm, his eyes flicking toward the door.

"Who's there?" he barked, his voice echoing through the sterile hallway.

Footsteps clicked against the polished tiles, growing louder, closer. Grace's breath caught in her throat as a familiar figure emerged from the shadows.

It was Dr. Wallace.

His sharp, calculating eyes swept over the scene, lingering on the struggling David before settling on Grace. His expression flickered – a momentary crack in his usually stoic mask.

"Dr. Wallace?" Grace stammered, her mind struggling to process this new twist. "What... what are you doing here?"

Wallace's eyes hardened, his jaw tightening as he took a step forward.

"David called me," he said, his voice cold and precise. "He said there was a... situation."

Grace's heart pounded in her chest, a fresh wave of betrayal flooding her veins. She took a step back, her mind racing, her gaze darting between David's twisted grin and Wallace's unreadable face.

"You knew?" she whispered, her voice trembling. "You've been in on this the whole time?"

Wallace's lips curled into a small, grim smile.

"Not the whole time," he said, his eyes locking onto hers. "But long enough to know that you've been digging too deep, Grace."

Grace felt her knees weaken, the room spinning around her.

"No," she breathed, her mind struggling to piece together this fresh betrayal. "This can't be... You were my friend... my mentor."

Wallace's expression remained cold, his eyes flicking briefly to Marcus, still holding David in a bruising grip.

"You never understood, Grace," Wallace said, his tone tinged with a twisted sense of pity. "Some of us see the world for what it really is – a game of control and power. And you... you were just a piece on the board."

Before she could react, Wallace reached into his coat, pulling out a sleek, black handgun, its polished barrel glinting in the dim light.

Grace froze, her breath catching in her throat as Wallace leveled the gun at her chest, his eyes cold and unfeeling.

Marcus's grip on David loosened for a split second, his eyes widening in shock.

"Wallace," he growled, his voice low and dangerous, "put the gun down."

Wallace's thin lips curled into a cruel smile.

"Sorry, Marcus," he said, his finger tightening on the trigger. "But this is where your little crusade ends."

The cold barrel of Wallace's gun gleamed under the flickering fluorescent lights, its dark, unforgiving gaze fixed on Grace's chest. The sharp, metallic scent of gun oil mixed with the sterile tang of antiseptic, filling the small, claustrophobic office.

David, still twisted in Marcus's grasp, let out a low, guttural laugh, his eyes gleaming with twisted satisfaction.

"You see, Grace," he hissed, his breath coming in short, manic bursts, "you were always out of your depth."

Grace felt her pulse racing, her heartbeat pounding in her ears, each thud echoing the ticking seconds of her life slipping away. She forced herself to meet Wallace's icy stare, her mind scrambling for a way out, a desperate plan forming in the chaos of her fear.

"You don't have to do this," she whispered, her eyes darting between Wallace's stony face and the barrel of the gun. "Think about your family. Your career. This isn't you."

Wallace's jaw tightened, a flicker of doubt flashing in his eyes before his expression hardened again.

"Don't try to psychoanalyze me, Grace," he snapped, his finger twitching against the trigger. "You have no idea what I've sacrificed for this... for him." He shot a glance at David, whose grin only grew wider, his teeth flashing like a predator sensing blood.

Marcus's grip tightened on David's arm, his muscles straining as he tried to calculate his next move. He knew one wrong step could end in a bloodbath.

"Wallace, listen to her," Marcus said, his voice a low, urgent growl. "This doesn't have to end like this. Put the gun down. We can still fix this."

Wallace's eyes flicked toward Marcus, a flicker of something – regret? – flashing in his eyes before vanishing behind a cold, calculated mask.

"Fix this?" he echoed, his voice dripping with bitter amusement. "There's nothing left to fix. This world belongs to those with the will to seize it. And the two of you... you're just obstacles."

In that split second, Grace's mind flashed back to the countless conversations she'd had with Wallace over the years – the late-night strategy sessions, the debates about ethics, the moments when he'd seemed so deeply invested in her success. She'd trusted him. She'd seen him as a mentor, even a friend.

But now, she realized, she'd been nothing more than a pawn in his twisted game.

Suddenly, the silence was shattered by a loud crash from the hallway – the sound of glass breaking, followed by frantic footsteps and a muffled scream. Wallace's head snapped toward the door, his gun lowering by a fraction as his instincts kicked in. Grace seized the moment.

With a surge of adrenaline, she lunged forward, grabbing the heavy ceramic paperweight from the desk and swinging it with all her strength. It connected with Wallace's wrist with a sickening crack, the gun clattering to the floor as he let out a strangled cry of pain.

Marcus reacted instantly, shoving David into the desk and diving for the gun. David stumbled, his face slamming into the corner of the desk with a sharp, wet crunch, a spray of blood splattering the polished wood.

Wallace staggered back, clutching his shattered wrist, his eyes wide with shock and fury.

"You... you stupid, naive—" he spat, his words cut off as Marcus sprang to his feet, the gun now firmly in his grip, its barrel aimed squarely at Wallace's chest.

"Move, and I'll end you," Marcus snarled, his finger curling around the trigger, his chest heaving with rage.

Grace backed away, her heart still racing, her eyes darting between the two men as the chaos of the moment settled into a tense, dangerous standoff.

David, still dazed and bleeding from the gash on his forehead, pushed himself up from the desk, his eyes wild, his mouth twisted into a snarl.

"You have no idea what you've just done," he spat, wiping the blood from his eyes. "You think this is over? It's just beginning."

The door burst open, and two police officers stormed into the room, their guns drawn, their eyes wide with shock as they took in the chaotic scene.

"Drop the weapon!" one of them shouted, his gaze locked on Marcus, his hands steady as he aimed his pistol.

Marcus hesitated, his eyes flicking to Grace, who stood frozen, her breath coming in short, panicked gasps.

"Marcus, please," Grace whispered, her voice trembling. "Don't make this worse. Just... let them handle it."

For a long, agonizing moment, Marcus's jaw clenched, his eyes blazing with a mixture of fury and heartbreak. Then, slowly, he lowered the gun, letting it clatter to the floor at his feet.

The officers moved in, one of them grabbing Marcus and forcing him against the wall, the other shoving Wallace to his knees, his broken wrist twisted awkwardly behind his back as he let out a low, guttural moan of pain.

David remained where he was, his chest heaving, his eyes locked on Grace, a twisted smile playing at his bloodied lips.

"This isn't over," he whispered, his voice a dark, ominous promise.

Grace felt the room spinning around her, the walls closing in as the weight of everything crashed down on her – the betrayal, the lies, the fear for her daughter's life.

And in that moment, she knew – this nightmare was far from over.

CHAPTER 18

Ghost from the past

The police officers moved swiftly, cuffing Wallace and dragging him to his feet. His face twisted in a mixture of pain and pure, unadulterated rage as he spat curses at Grace and Marcus. The fluorescent lights cast harsh, unforgiving shadows on his crumpled form, illuminating the depth of his madness.

David, still bleeding from his forehead, remained slumped against the desk, his breath coming in ragged, furious gasps. His eyes burned into Grace's, a silent, venomous promise hanging between them.

As the officers began reading Wallace his rights, one of them paused, his head cocked as if he had just received a message through his earpiece. His eyes widened for a fraction of a second, then he turned to his partner, nodding grimly.

"We need to get them both to the station," he said, tightening his grip on Wallace's cuffs. "Now."

They began dragging Wallace toward the door, his broken wrist hanging at an odd angle, his face a mask of agony and hatred.

"Grace," he hissed as they pulled him past her, his voice low and dripping with malice. "You've just destroyed everything. You have no idea what you've unleashed."

Grace felt a shiver run down her spine, her mind racing as she tried to make sense of his words.

As soon as the door slammed shut behind the officers, Marcus collapsed onto the nearest chair, his face pale, his hands still trembling from the adrenaline crash. He dropped his head into his hands, his breath coming in short, ragged gasps.

Grace took a step toward him, her own heart still thundering in her chest.

"Marcus," she whispered, her voice hoarse, "what the hell just happened? Why was Wallace... why did he—"

Marcus looked up at her, his eyes bloodshot, his face etched with a mix of regret and exhaustion.

"Grace," he said, his voice barely more than a whisper, "we've stumbled into something much bigger than we thought. Wallace... he wasn't just protecting David. He was covering up something much darker."

Grace felt a cold knot of fear tighten in her stomach, her mind flashing back to the strange calls, the encrypted messages, the whispers in the hospital corridors.

"What do you mean?" she demanded, her voice trembling. "What else is going on?"

Marcus leaned back, running a shaky hand through his hair, his eyes flicking to the door as if expecting Wallace to burst back in at any moment.

"Wallace and David," he said slowly, "weren't just involved in some affair or financial scam. It's deeper. Much deeper."

Grace felt her breath catch in her throat, a sickening wave of dread washing over her.

"What are you talking about?" she whispered, her hands clenching into fists at her sides.

Marcus's eyes locked onto hers, his jaw tightening.

"Wallace has been part of a secret network," he said, his voice dropping to a low, urgent whisper. "A group of influential people – doctors, politicians, businessmen – all connected through a shadow organization. They manipulate patients, influence court cases, control media narratives. It's all about power and control. And David... he's one of their pawns."

Grace felt her knees go weak, her mind struggling to process the words.

"No," she whispered, shaking her head. "That can't be true. David... he's a liar, a cheat, but he's not... he's not part of something like that."

Marcus gave a bitter, humorless laugh, his eyes dark with a twisted kind of understanding.

"You'd be surprised what people are capable of when they're desperate," he said, leaning forward, his eyes boring into hers. "And Wallace... he was willing to kill to keep this secret."

Grace felt the room spin around her, her vision blurring as the weight of Marcus's words crashed down on her.

"But... why? Why would Wallace risk everything for this? What does he stand to gain?"

Marcus hesitated, his jaw working as he struggled to find the right words.

"Wallace has connections," he said finally, his voice grim. "High-level connections. He's not just a doctor. He's a fixer – a man who cleans up messes for powerful people. And David... he's more than just a pawn. He's a key piece in their game."

Grace staggered back, her mind reeling, her breath coming in shallow, panicked gasps.

"You mean... this was never just about us?" she whispered, her eyes wide with horror. "This was about power... about control?"

Marcus nodded slowly, his face pale, his eyes hollow.

"And now," he said, his voice trembling, "we're right in the middle of it."

The words hung in the air between them, heavy with the weight of a terrible, dawning realization.

Grace felt a cold, suffocating dread creep over her, the walls of the small office closing in around her. She had thought she was fighting for her marriage, her family, her sanity.

But now, she realized, she was fighting for her life.

Grace sat alone in the dimly lit kitchen, the only sound the slow, rhythmic ticking of the wall clock. Her hands clutched a cup of lukewarm tea, her mind racing, her heart pounding with a chaotic mix of fear and fury. Marcus's words still echoed in her head, twisting and warping her reality.

Wallace... part of a secret network. David... a key piece in their game.

She felt like she was losing her grip on everything she thought she knew. The man she had married, the man she had loved and cared for, was not just a liar or a cheat. He was part of something far more sinister.

The sound of the front door creaking open snapped her out of her spiraling thoughts. She stiffened, her muscles tensing, her heart hammering in her chest as David's footsteps echoed through the hallway.

"Grace?" he called, his voice sounding too calm, too controlled. He paused at the entrance to the kitchen, his shadow stretching long and distorted across the tiled floor.

She looked up, her eyes locking onto his, and for a fleeting moment, she saw the man she had once loved. The man who had held her close on their wedding night, whispered promises of forever in her ear. But that man felt like a distant memory now – a ghost of the past, overshadowed by the stranger standing before her.

"You're still up?" he said, his eyes narrowing slightly as he took in her rigid posture and clenched jaw.

Grace forced a brittle, bitter smile onto her lips, setting down her cup with a soft clink.

"Couldn't sleep," she replied, her voice steady but laced with an icy edge. "Had a lot on my mind."

David hesitated, a flicker of something like uncertainty passing over his face. He took a step closer, his eyes searching hers for a hint of weakness, a crack in her armor.

"Is everything alright?" he asked, his tone carefully measured, his head tilting just slightly as if trying to gauge her emotional state.

Grace met his gaze head-on, her pulse throbbing in her ears.

"You tell me," she said, her voice low and challenging. "Should everything be alright, David?"

He froze for a split second, his eyes flicking to the side before he quickly forced a smile.

"Of course," he said, his voice a touch too bright, too rehearsed. "Why wouldn't it be?"

Grace felt a surge of anger flare up inside her, her hands tightening into fists beneath the table. She could feel the cracks spreading, the fragile mask of their marriage beginning to shatter around them.

"Because I'm not blind, David," she whispered, leaning forward, her eyes boring into his. "Not anymore."

David's face went pale, his body tensing, his jaw clenching so hard she could see the muscles twitch beneath his skin.

"What... what do you mean?" he stammered, his voice losing its practiced calm, his eyes darting around the room as if searching for an escape.

Grace felt a twisted, bitter satisfaction at his sudden panic, the thrill of catching a predator in his own trap.

"I know," she said, her voice dropping to a dangerous whisper, her eyes never leaving his. "About you. About Wallace. About the lies. The secrets."

David took a stumbling step back, his breath coming in sharp, shallow gasps. For a moment, she thought he might collapse right there in the kitchen, his carefully constructed facade crumbling beneath the weight of her words.

"Grace, you... you don't understand," he stammered, his hands trembling as he reached for the counter, his knuckles turning white as he gripped the edge. "It's... it's complicated."

Grace let out a sharp, humorless laugh, the sound echoing off the cold kitchen tiles.

"Complicated?" she spat, rising to her feet, her eyes blazing with a fury she hadn't felt in years. "You think that justifies everything you've done? The lies, the deceit, the manipulation?"

David's mouth opened and closed like a fish gasping for air, his eyes wide, his face ashen. He looked like a man standing on the edge of a cliff, staring down into the abyss, his secrets threatening to pull him under.

"Grace, please," he whispered, his voice breaking, his eyes filled with a raw, desperate fear. "I can explain. Just... just give me a chance."

Grace felt a twisted, vindictive pleasure at his panic, a deep, primal satisfaction at seeing him squirm. But beneath the anger, beneath the righteous fury, there was a hollow ache, a deep, festering wound that threatened to consume her.

"Explain?" she snarled, taking a step toward him, her eyes blazing. "Then go ahead, David. Explain to me why you've been lying to me for years. Why you've been using me, manipulating me, playing me like a fool."

David stumbled back, his hands shaking, his eyes wide with a terror she had never seen before.

"Grace," he whispered, his voice trembling, his body shaking. "I... I never meant for this to happen. I never wanted you to find out. I was... I was trying to protect you."

She felt her blood turn to ice, her breath catching in her throat.

"Protect me?" she spat, her voice dripping with venom. "From what, David? From the truth? From you?"

David's face twisted into a mask of despair, his body crumpling against the counter, his head dropping into his hands.

"From them," he whispered, his voice broken, his eyes brimming with tears. "From the people who will come for you if they find out you know."

Grace felt her blood run cold, her mind racing as his words crashed over her like a tidal wave.

Them.

She took a shaky step back, her heart pounding, her mind reeling.

"What... what have you done, David?" she whispered, her voice barely more than a breath, her eyes wide with terror.

David slowly raised his head, his eyes hollow, his face etched with a haunting, bone-deep fear.

"I've made a deal," he whispered, his voice shaking. "A deal I can't break."

Grace felt the floor drop out from beneath her, the room spinning around her as the full, horrifying truth crashed down on her.

And for the first time in her life, she realized that she might not survive this nightmare.

David's confession hung in the air like a noxious cloud, choking the breath from Grace's lungs. She staggered back, her mind reeling, her body trembling as the weight of his words crashed over her.

"A deal?" she whispered, her voice barely more than a breath, her heart thundering in her chest. "What kind of deal, David?"

David's eyes, bloodshot and haunted, locked onto hers. He looked like a man standing on the edge of a precipice, the ground crumbling beneath his feet.

"It's... it's not what you think," he stammered, his voice trembling, his hands shaking as he reached for her. "I was... I was desperate. I didn't have a choice."

Grace took a shaky step back, her mind racing, her heart pounding. She felt like a cornered animal, her every instinct screaming at her to run, to get as far away from him as possible.

"Don't," she spat, her eyes blazing with a wild, terrified fury. "Don't touch me."

David froze, his hands dropping to his sides, his face crumpling in despair.

"Grace, please," he whispered, his voice breaking. "I... I can explain."

She let out a harsh, bitter laugh, the sound echoing off the cold kitchen tiles.

"Explain?" she snarled, her eyes narrowing into furious slits. "Explain what, David? That you've been lying to me for years? That you've been playing me for a fool? That you've been hiding things from me?"

David's face twisted in pain, his body trembling as he leaned heavily against the counter, his head dropping into his hands.

"It's more complicated than that," he whispered, his voice muffled, his shoulders shaking.

Grace felt a fresh wave of rage wash over her, her hands clenching into fists, her nails digging into her palms.

"Then make me understand," she hissed, her voice laced with venom. "Make me understand why you've been lying to me, why you've been hiding things from me."

David looked up, his eyes hollow, his face etched with a bone-deep fear that sent a chill racing down her spine.

"I did it for us," he whispered, his voice breaking, his eyes brimming with tears. "I did it to protect you."

Grace felt a bitter, twisted laugh bubble up in her throat, her body shaking with rage.

"Protect me?" she spat, her eyes blazing. "From what, David? From the truth? From you?"

David's face crumpled, his body collapsing against the counter, his head dropping into his hands.

"No," he whispered, his voice trembling. "From him."

Grace felt her blood run cold, her breath catching in her throat.

"Him?" she whispered, her voice barely more than a breath, her eyes wide with terror. "Who is 'him,' David?"

David slowly raised his head, his eyes hollow, his face etched with a haunting, bone-deep fear.

"A man I thought I'd never see again," he whispered, his voice shaking. "A man I thought was gone for good."

Grace felt a cold, nauseating dread coil in the pit of her stomach, her heart pounding, her mind racing.

"Who?" she whispered, her voice trembling, her hands shaking. "Who is he, David?"

David's eyes dropped to the floor, his shoulders slumping, his body trembling.

"His name is Viktor," he whispered, his voice hollow, his eyes filled with a raw, desperate fear. "Viktor Razin."

Grace felt her knees go weak, her vision swimming, her body swaying on the spot.

"Viktor Razin?" she whispered, her voice shaking, her heart pounding. "Who... who is he?"

David let out a harsh, bitter laugh, the sound echoing off the cold kitchen tiles.

"He's the man who made me who I am," he whispered, his voice trembling, his eyes brimming with tears. "The man who saved my life... and destroyed it."

Grace felt a fresh wave of terror crash over her, her mind reeling, her heart pounding.

"David," she whispered, her voice trembling, her hands shaking.

"What... what have you done?"

David's head dropped into his hands, his shoulders shaking, his body crumpling against the counter.

"I made a deal with the devil," he whispered, his voice breaking, his eyes brimming with tears. "And now he's come to collect."

CHAPTER 19

Whispers of the Past

The kitchen felt like a prison, the air thick with the sharp scent of fear and desperation. Grace's mind spun, the pieces of David's confession clashing violently in her head. Viktor Razin. The name echoed in her mind, dark and menacing, dripping with danger.

"Who is this Viktor?" she demanded, her voice trembling, her hands clenching into tight fists. "What kind of man are you mixed up with, David?"

David's shoulders slumped, his eyes distant, as if he were staring into the abyss of his past. He looked broken, the weight of his secrets pressing down on him, threatening to crush him.

"He's... he's a ghost, Grace," David whispered, his voice hollow, his eyes haunted. "A ghost from a past I thought I'd buried."

Grace took a step closer, her heart racing, her breath coming in short, sharp gasps. She felt like she was teetering on the edge of a cliff, the ground crumbling beneath her feet.

"A ghost?" she whispered, her voice shaking. "What do you mean, David? What have you done?"

David closed his eyes, his body trembling, his fists clenching at his sides. He felt the weight of her gaze, the sharp, accusing eyes that had once looked at him with love, now filled with fear and betrayal.

"It was years ago," he whispered, his voice breaking, his head dropping into his hands. "Before the accident, before... before you."

Grace's heart skipped a beat, her mind racing, her pulse pounding in her ears.

"What did you do, David?" she whispered, her voice trembling, her hands shaking. "What did you do?"

David took a deep, shuddering breath, his body trembling, his eyes brimming with tears.

"I made a deal," he whispered, his voice hollow, his eyes distant. "A deal I thought I could walk away from. But you don't walk away from Viktor Razin. You don't walk away from the devil."

Grace felt a cold, nauseating dread coil in the pit of her stomach, her heart pounding, her mind racing. She took a shaky step back, her body trembling, her breath coming in short, sharp gasps.

"You... you made a deal with a criminal?" she whispered, her voice shaking, her eyes wide with terror.

David let out a harsh, bitter laugh, the sound echoing off the cold kitchen tiles.

"He wasn't just a criminal," he whispered, his voice trembling, his eyes hollow. "He was a kingpin, a monster. A man who thrived on fear, on chaos, on blood."

Grace felt a cold sweat break out across her skin, her mind spinning, her heart racing. She felt like she was drowning, her lungs burning, her body trembling.

"Why, David?" she whispered, her voice breaking, her eyes brimming with tears. "Why would you do that?"

David's head dropped into his hands, his shoulders shaking, his body crumpling against the counter.

"I had no choice," he whispered, his voice breaking, his eyes brimming with tears. "I was young, desperate, drowning in debt. I needed a way out, a way to escape."

Grace felt a bitter, twisted laugh bubble up in her throat, her body shaking with rage.

"So you turned to a criminal?" she spat, her eyes blazing, her hands clenching into fists. "You sold your soul to a monster?"

David's face twisted in pain, his body trembling, his fists clenching at his sides.

"I thought I could walk away," he whispered, his voice breaking, his eyes brimming with tears. "I thought I could escape."

Grace felt a fresh wave of terror crash over her, her mind reeling, her heart pounding.

"But you didn't," she whispered, her voice trembling, her hands shaking. "You didn't escape."

David slowly raised his head, his eyes hollow, his face etched with a haunting, bone-deep fear.

"No," he whispered, his voice trembling, his eyes brimming with tears. "I didn't."

Later that night...

Grace sat alone in the darkened living room, her mind racing, her heart pounding. She felt like she was drowning, her lungs burning, her body trembling. She couldn't stop thinking about David's confession, about the dark, twisted past he had tried so hard to bury.

As she sat there, the shadows creeping across the walls, the silence pressing down on her, she heard a soft rustling outside the window. She froze, her heart skipping a beat, her breath catching in her throat.

Slowly, she rose from the couch, her body trembling, her heart racing. She crept towards the window, her bare feet whispering against the cool wooden floor, her breath coming in short, sharp gasps.

She reached the window, her hands shaking, her heart pounding, and slowly pulled back the curtain.

Her blood ran cold.

There, standing in the shadows, his face hidden by the dark, was a figure, tall and broad-shouldered, his eyes glowing in the moonlight.

For a moment, their eyes met, a silent, terrifying connection sparking between them.

Then, as quickly as he had appeared, the figure melted back into the shadows, disappearing into the night.

Grace staggered back, her body trembling, her breath coming in short, sharp gasps.

Who was he?

Was this Viktor?

Or was it someone else, someone even more dangerous?

The moon hung low in the sky, casting a pale, ghostly glow over the quiet street. The wind whispered through the trees, their branches swaying like twisted, skeletal fingers, casting long, eerie shadows across the lawn.

Grace sat on the edge of the bed, her mind racing, her heart pounding. She felt like a stranger in her own home, the walls pressing in on her, the air thick with the suffocating weight of secrets and lies.

David was in the shower, the sound of the water echoing through the walls, a steady, rhythmic beat that seemed to match the frantic pounding of her heart. She could still see the haunted look in his eyes, the fear, the regret, the darkness.

A criminal.

He had made a deal with a monster, sold his soul to a devil, and now that devil had come to collect.

Grace's mind spun, her thoughts tumbling over each other like jagged shards of broken glass. She felt a cold, nauseating dread coil in the pit of her stomach, her body trembling, her breath coming in short, sharp gasps.

Flashback – Ten Years Ago

David sat in the dimly lit bar, his hands trembling, his heart pounding. The air was thick with the heavy, bitter scent of stale beer and cigarette smoke, the low, murmured conversations around him blending into a chaotic, suffocating hum.

He took a long, shaky sip of his drink, the harsh, burning liquid searing his throat, his mind spinning.

He had hit rock bottom.

The debt collectors were circling like vultures, their cold, calculating eyes fixed on him, their sharp, greedy talons ready to tear him apart. His business was failing, his finances in ruins, his life crumbling around him.

And then, like a dark, twisted miracle, Viktor Razin had appeared.

The man had slid into the seat across from him, his sharp, predatory eyes fixed on David, his thin, cruel lips curling into a cold, calculating smile.

"I hear you're in a bit of a bind, David," he had said, his voice low, smooth, dripping with false sympathy. "Perhaps I can help."

David had felt a cold sweat break out across his skin, his heart skipping a beat, his mind racing.

"I... I don't know what you're talking about," he had stammered, his hands shaking, his breath coming in short, sharp gasps.

Viktor had chuckled, a dark, bone-chilling sound that sent a shiver down David's spine.

"Come now, David," he had said, leaning in closer, his sharp, predatory eyes glinting in the dim light. "You're drowning, my friend. And I... I'm a very good swimmer."

David had felt a cold, nauseating dread coil in the pit of his stomach, his body trembling, his heart pounding.

"What do you want?" he had whispered, his voice shaking, his eyes wide with fear.

Viktor had leaned back in his seat, his thin, cruel lips curling into a satisfied smile.

"Oh, nothing much," he had said, his voice low, smooth, dripping with menace. "Just a small favor. A little... insurance, if you will."

David had felt his heart skip a beat, his mind spinning, his pulse pounding in his ears.

"What kind of insurance?" he had whispered, his voice trembling, his hands shaking.

Viktor's smile had widened, his sharp, predatory eyes glinting with a dark, twisted amusement.

"Oh, you'll find out soon enough," he had said, his voice low, smooth, dripping with menace. "But for now, let's just say that you owe me. And I always collect."

Back to the Present

Grace snapped back to the present, her heart racing, her breath coming in short, sharp gasps. She felt like she was drowning, her lungs burning, her body trembling. She couldn't stop thinking about David's confession, about the dark, twisted past he had tried so hard to bury.

She glanced towards the bathroom door, the sound of the water still echoing through the walls, a steady, rhythmic beat that seemed to match the frantic pounding of her heart.

She had to know more. She had to understand.

Without a second thought, she grabbed her phone and dialed Dr. Wallace's number, her hands trembling, her breath coming in short, sharp gasps.

The phone rang once, twice, three times, before the familiar, warm voice crackled through the line.

"Grace?" Dr. Wallace's voice sounded surprised, a hint of concern creeping into his tone. "Is everything okay?"

Grace took a deep, shuddering breath, her body trembling, her mind racing.

"Dr. Wallace," she whispered, her voice shaking, her eyes brimming with tears. "I... I need to talk to you. It's about David."

There was a long, heavy silence on the other end of the line, the air thick with tension, the unspoken fears and doubts hanging between them like a dark, suffocating cloud.

"Alright," Dr. Wallace finally said, his voice low, calm, reassuring. "Meet me at my office in an hour."

Grace felt a fresh wave of fear crash over her, her heart racing, her mind spinning. She glanced towards the bathroom door, the sound of the water still echoing through the walls, a steady, rhythmic beat that seemed to match the frantic pounding of her heart.

"I'll be there," she whispered, her voice trembling, her hands shaking.

She ended the call, her body trembling, her breath coming in short, sharp gasps.

This was it. The moment of truth.

She had to know. She had to understand.

And she wasn't sure she was ready for what she might find.

Grace stepped out into the cool night air, her mind spinning, her heart racing. The street was quiet, the distant hum of traffic a dull, ever-present murmur in the background. She pulled her coat tighter around her, the cold biting at her skin, her breath coming in short, sharp gasps, misting in the icy air.

Her mind was a chaotic, swirling storm of fear, doubt, and anger.

She felt like a woman on the edge of a cliff, the ground crumbling beneath her feet, the abyss yawning wide and dark below. She had to know the truth. She had to understand.

Dr. Wallace's office was only a few blocks away, the path familiar, the shadows long and twisted in the dim, flickering streetlights. She walked quickly, her footsteps echoing off the cold, hard pavement, her heart pounding in her chest, her mind racing.

As she rounded the corner onto the main street, her eyes caught a dark, sleek car parked across from the small, nondescript building where Dr. Wallace's office was located. The engine was still running, the faint, bluish glow of the dashboard lights casting eerie shadows across the tinted windows.

A chill ran down her spine, her heart skipping a beat. She slowed her steps, her eyes narrowing, her breath coming in short, sharp gasps. Something about that car felt wrong, felt dangerous, felt... familiar.

And then she saw him.

A tall, thin figure, wrapped in a long, dark coat, leaning against the car, his sharp, predatory eyes fixed on the entrance to Dr. Wallace's office. The dim streetlight cast long, twisted shadows across his angular features, his thin lips curled into a cold, calculating smile.

Viktor Razin.

Grace felt a fresh wave of fear crash over her, her body trembling, her mind spinning. She ducked into the shadows of a nearby alley, her breath coming in short, sharp gasps, her heart pounding in her chest.

What was he doing here? Had he followed her? Was this a coincidence? Or was this something more, something darker, something more dangerous?

She pressed her back against the cold, damp brick wall, her eyes fixed on the shadowy figure across the street, her mind racing, her pulse pounding in her ears. She had to think, she had to stay calm, she had to...

The door to Dr. Wallace's office creaked open, the sound echoing down the empty street, sharp and harsh against the cold, silent night. Grace held her breath, her eyes wide, her heart racing.

Dr. Wallace stepped out into the dim, flickering light, his face pale, his eyes wide, his body tense, his movements stiff and awkward. He glanced nervously up and down the street, his hands shaking, his breath coming in short, sharp gasps, misting in the icy air.

Viktor straightened, his sharp, predatory eyes fixed on the old man, his thin, cruel lips curling into a satisfied smile.

"Dr. Wallace," he said, his voice low, smooth, dripping with menace, his words cutting through the cold night air like a knife. "We need to talk."

Dr. Wallace froze, his eyes wide, his body trembling, his heart pounding in his chest. He took a shaky step back, his breath coming in short, sharp gasps, his mind spinning.

"Viktor... I... I don't..." he stammered, his voice shaking, his hands trembling.

Viktor took a slow, deliberate step forward, his sharp, predatory eyes never leaving the old man's face, his thin, cruel lips curling into a cold, calculating smile.

"You know what this is about, doctor," he said, his voice low, smooth, dripping with menace. "You know exactly what this is about."

Grace felt a fresh wave of fear crash over her, her body trembling, her breath coming in short, sharp gasps. She pressed herself deeper into the shadows, her heart pounding, her mind racing.

This was it. The moment of truth.

She had to know. She had to understand.

And she wasn't sure she was ready for what she might find.

CHAPTER 20

Dance with the Devil

Grace's breath hitched as she pressed herself harder against the cold, damp brick wall. She felt the icy moisture seeping into her coat, chilling her to the bone, but she barely noticed. Her pulse was a relentless drumbeat in her ears, her mind racing, her heart pounding.

Viktor took another step toward Dr. Wallace, his sharp, predatory eyes narrowing, his thin, cruel lips curling into a sinister smile.

"Don't play games with me, Wallace," he said, his voice low, smooth, dripping with menace. "You know exactly what this is about."

Dr. Wallace took a shaky step back, his eyes wide, his body trembling. He glanced nervously up and down the empty street, his breath coming in short, sharp gasps, misting in the icy air.

"I... I don't know what you're talking about, Viktor," he stammered, his voice shaking, his hands trembling. "I'm just a doctor... I don't... I don't know anything..."

Viktor's smile widened, his sharp, predatory eyes never leaving the old man's face.

"Lies," he said, his voice a cold, sharp whisper, his words cutting through the silent night like a knife. "I can smell the fear on you, Wallace. I can taste it."

Grace felt her heart lurch in her chest, her breath catching in her throat. She clenched her fists, her nails digging into her palms, her mind spinning.

What was this? What was Viktor doing here? What did he want from Dr. Wallace? And what did this have to do with David, with her, with the tangled, twisted web of lies and deceit that had become her life?

Viktor took another step forward, his sharp, predatory eyes narrowing, his thin, cruel lips curling into a sinister smile.

"You've been talking, Wallace," he said, his voice low, smooth, dripping with menace. "And I don't like it when people talk."

Dr. Wallace's eyes went wide, his breath coming in short, sharp gasps, his body trembling. He took another shaky step back, his hands shaking, his heart pounding in his chest.

"I... I haven't said anything, Viktor," he stammered, his voice shaking, his hands trembling. "I swear... I haven't said anything..."

Viktor's smile widened, his sharp, predatory eyes never leaving the old man's face.

"Lies," he said, his voice a cold, sharp whisper, his words cutting through the silent night like a knife. "You're lying, Wallace. I can see it in your eyes."

Grace felt a fresh wave of fear crash over her, her body trembling, her breath coming in short, sharp gasps. She pressed herself deeper into the shadows, her heart pounding, her mind racing.

And then, without warning, Dr. Wallace stumbled back, his foot catching on the edge of the curb, his body lurching backward, his arms flailing wildly. He let out a sharp, panicked cry, his eyes wide, his breath coming in short, sharp gasps.

Grace felt her heart lurch in her chest, her breath catching in her throat.

Dr. Wallace stumbled back again, his arms flailing, his eyes wide, his breath coming in short, sharp gasps. He crashed into the garbage cans behind him, the sharp, metallic clatter echoing down the empty street, sharp and harsh against the cold, silent night.

Viktor's sharp, predatory eyes flicked toward the noise, his thin, cruel lips curling into a cold, calculating smile.

Grace felt her heart skip a beat, her breath catching in her throat. She ducked deeper into the shadows, her body trembling, her mind racing, her heart pounding in her chest.

Viktor took a slow, deliberate step toward the alley where Grace was hiding, his sharp, predatory eyes narrowing, his thin, cruel lips curling into a cold, calculating smile.

Grace held her breath, her eyes wide, her heart pounding in her chest.

Was this it? Had he seen her? Had he heard her?

She felt her pulse quicken, her breath coming in short, sharp gasps, her mind racing.

And then, just as suddenly as he had turned, Viktor's eyes flicked back to Dr. Wallace, his thin, cruel lips curling into a cold, calculating smile.

"Be careful, Wallace," he said, his voice low, smooth, dripping with menace. "Accidents happen."

Dr. Wallace staggered back, his breath coming in short, sharp gasps, his body trembling. He glanced nervously up and down the empty street, his heart pounding in his chest, his mind racing.

"I... I understand, Viktor," he stammered, his voice shaking, his hands trembling. "I... I won't say anything... I promise..."

Viktor smiled, his sharp, predatory eyes narrowing, his thin, cruel lips curling into a cold, calculating smile.

"Good," he said, his voice a cold, sharp whisper, his words cutting through the silent night like a knife. "Because if you do... I'll know."

And with that, he turned, his long, dark coat swirling around him, his sharp, predatory eyes never leaving Dr. Wallace's face. He took a slow, deliberate step back toward his car, his thin, cruel lips curling into a cold, calculating smile.

Dr. Wallace stood frozen, his eyes wide, his breath coming in short, sharp gasps, his body trembling.

And then, without another word, Viktor slipped into his car, the engine roaring to life, the headlights cutting through the darkness, the sleek, black vehicle sliding smoothly down the empty street, disappearing into the night.

Grace let out a shaky breath, her heart pounding, her mind spinning. She felt like a woman on the edge of a cliff, the ground crumbling beneath her feet, the abyss yawning wide and dark below.

She had to know. She had to understand.

And she wasn't sure she was ready for what she might find.

CHAPTER 21

The Cracks in the Mask

Grace waited for her heart to stop racing before slipping out of the alley. She clutched her coat tightly around her, the cold seeping into her bones, her breath misting in the night air. She cast a quick glance down the street where Viktor's car had disappeared, then turned her gaze back to Dr. Wallace.

He was still there, leaning against the grimy brick wall, his chest heaving, his hands trembling, his eyes wide with terror. His thin, grey hair clung to his damp forehead, and his wire-rimmed glasses were askew, one lens cracked, giving him a wild, unhinged look.

For a moment, Grace hesitated. She felt a pang of sympathy for the old man, his frail frame trembling, his wide, terrified eyes darting back and forth like a cornered animal.

But then the image of David flickered in her mind – his lies, his betrayal, his twisted games – and her sympathy hardened into resolve.

She stepped out of the shadows, her heels clicking sharply against the wet pavement, her breath coming in short, determined puffs.

Dr. Wallace's head snapped up, his bloodshot eyes locking onto her. For a moment, he just stared, his mouth working soundlessly, his eyes wide with terror.

"Dr. Wallace," Grace said, her voice low, sharp, her eyes blazing. "We need to talk."

Wallace's eyes went even wider, his breath catching in his throat. He took a shaky step back, his frail, trembling hands gripping the edge of the brick wall behind him.

"G-Grace?" he stammered, his voice weak, his body trembling. "What... what are you doing here?"

Grace took another step forward, her heels clicking sharply against the pavement, her eyes narrowing, her jaw tightening.

"I could ask you the same thing," she said, her voice cold, sharp, each word a dagger. "Why are you meeting with Viktor in the shadows like some kind of cornered rat?"

Wallace's face drained of color, his breath coming in short, sharp gasps, his eyes wide with terror. He took another shaky step back, his thin, frail body pressing against the cold, damp brick wall.

"I... I don't know what you're talking about," he stammered, his voice shaking, his hands trembling. "I... I'm just... I was just..."

"Save it," Grace snapped, her eyes blazing, her jaw tightening. "I heard everything. I saw everything. I know you're hiding something, Wallace. I know you're involved in this... this twisted game that David's been playing."

Wallace's eyes flicked nervously up and down the empty street, his breath coming in short, sharp gasps, his thin, frail body trembling.

"I... I can't..." he stammered, his voice weak, his eyes wide, his hands trembling. "I can't... I can't talk about this... it's... it's not safe..."

Grace felt a fresh wave of anger surge through her, her fists clenching, her teeth grinding. She took another step forward, her heels clicking sharply against the pavement, her eyes narrowing, her jaw tightening.

"Not safe?" she hissed, her voice low, sharp, her eyes blazing. "You're worried about your safety? After what you've put me through? After what you've put my family through?"

Wallace flinched, his eyes wide, his breath coming in short, sharp gasps, his thin, frail body trembling.

"I... I didn't mean for any of this to happen," he stammered, his voice shaking, his eyes wide, his hands trembling. "I... I never wanted... I never thought it would go this far..."

Grace felt her pulse quicken, her breath coming in short, sharp gasps, her mind racing. She took another step forward, her heels clicking sharply against the pavement, her eyes narrowing, her jaw tightening.

"Then tell me the truth," she snapped, her voice low, sharp, her eyes blazing. "Tell me what you know. Tell me what you and Viktor are hiding. Tell me what David's been hiding."

Wallace's eyes flicked nervously up and down the empty street, his breath coming in short, sharp gasps, his thin, frail body trembling.

"Then make me understand," she hissed, her voice low, sharp, her eyes blazing. "Because I'm not leaving until you tell me the truth. All of it."

Wallace's eyes flicked nervously up and down the empty street, his breath coming in short, sharp gasps, his thin, frail body trembling. He opened his mouth to speak, then snapped it shut again, his eyes wide, his breath coming in short, sharp gasps, his hands trembling.

Grace took another step forward, her heels clicking sharply against the pavement, her eyes narrowing, her jaw tightening.

"Tell me, Wallace," she snapped, her voice low, sharp, her eyes blazing. "Tell me what you know. Tell me what you're hiding. Tell me the truth."

Wallace's breath hitched, his eyes wide, his thin, frail body trembling. He glanced nervously up and down the empty street, his heart pounding in his chest, his mind racing.

And then, finally, he spoke.

"David... David isn't who you think he is," he whispered, his voice low, trembling, his eyes wide, his hands shaking. "He's... he's dangerous, Grace. More dangerous than you could ever imagine."

Grace felt her heart lurch in her chest, her breath catching in her throat, her mind spinning.

"What... what do you mean?" she whispered, her voice shaking, her eyes wide, her heart pounding in her chest.

Wallace glanced nervously up and down the empty street,

his breath coming in short, sharp gasps, his thin, frail body trembling.

"He's... he's not just a liar," he whispered, his voice low, trembling, his eyes wide, his hands shaking. "He's... he's a killer."

Grace stumbled back a step, the cold brick wall pressing into her spine as Dr. Wallace's words echoed in her mind.

A killer.

Her breath came in shallow, uneven gasps, her heart pounding so loudly she could hear it echoing in her ears. She gripped the wall behind her, her fingers pressing into the rough, damp bricks, her knees threatening to buckle beneath her.

"W-what are you talking about?" she stammered, her voice barely a whisper, her eyes wide, her pulse racing. "David... David's a lot of things, but he's not a killer. That's... that's insane."

Wallace's face twisted into a grimace, his eyes dark, haunted, his breath coming in short, sharp gasps. He glanced nervously up and down the empty alley, his thin, frail body trembling, his hands shaking.

"No," he whispered, his voice low, trembling, his eyes wide, his hands trembling. "It's not insane, Grace. It's the truth. The truth you've been blind to for too long."

Grace felt a fresh wave of nausea rise in her throat, her mind spinning, her heart racing. She clutched the brick wall behind her, her fingers digging into the rough, damp surface, her breath coming in short, shallow gasps.

"No," she whispered, shaking her head, her eyes wide, her heart pounding in her chest. "You're lying. You're trying to scare me. You're trying to manipulate me."

Wallace flinched, his eyes wide, his breath coming in short, sharp gasps, his thin, frail body trembling. He glanced nervously up and down the empty alley, his heart pounding in his chest, his mind racing.

"I'm not lying," he whispered, his voice low, trembling, his eyes wide, his hands trembling. "I wish I was. I wish I could tell you that this is all just some sick, twisted game. But it's not. It's real, Grace. It's real, and it's dangerous."

Grace felt her heart lurch in her chest, her breath catching in her throat, her mind spinning. She shook her head, her eyes wide, her heart pounding in her chest.

"No," she whispered, her voice shaking, her eyes wide, her heart racing. "You're lying. You're trying to confuse me, to manipulate me, to... to scare me into trusting you. But I won't. I won't fall for your lies."

Wallace's face twisted into a grimace, his eyes dark, haunted, his breath coming in short, sharp gasps. He took a shaky step forward, his thin, frail body trembling, his hands shaking.

"I'm not lying," he whispered, his voice low, trembling, his eyes wide, his hands trembling. "You have to believe me, Grace. You have to listen to me. Your life – and the lives of your children – depend on it."

Grace felt her blood run cold, her heart pounding in her chest, her breath coming in short, shallow gasps. She took a shaky step back, her back pressing harder against the cold brick wall behind her, her mind spinning, her pulse racing.

"What... what are you talking about?" she whispered, her voice shaking, her eyes wide, her heart pounding in her chest. "What do you mean my life depends on it?"

Wallace's eyes flicked nervously up and down the empty alley, his breath coming in short, sharp gasps, his thin, frail body trembling. He took another shaky step forward, his hands shaking, his eyes wide.

"I mean that David is dangerous," he whispered, his voice low, trembling, his eyes wide, his hands trembling. "More dangerous than you could ever imagine. He's not the man you think he is. He's not the man you married. He's... he's something else. Something dark. Something... monstrous."

Grace felt her heart lurch in her chest, her breath catching in her throat, her mind spinning. She clutched the brick wall behind her, her fingers digging into the rough, damp surface, her breath coming in short, shallow gasps.

"No," she whispered, her voice shaking, her eyes wide, her heart pounding in her chest. "You're lying. You're trying to manipulate me. You're trying to scare me."

Wallace's eyes flicked nervously up and down the empty alley, his breath coming in short, sharp gasps, his thin, frail body trembling. He took another shaky step forward, his hands shaking, his eyes wide.

"I'm not lying," he whispered, his voice low, trembling, his eyes wide, his hands trembling. "You have to believe me, Grace. You have to listen to me. Your life – and the lives of your children – depend on it."

Grace felt her blood run cold, her heart pounding in her chest, her breath coming in short, shallow gasps. She took a shaky step back, her back pressing harder against the cold brick wall behind her, her mind spinning, her pulse racing.

"Why... why should I believe you?" she whispered, her voice shaking, her eyes wide, her heart pounding in her chest. "Why should I trust you? You're a liar. You're a manipulator. You're... you're just as twisted as he is."

Wallace flinched, his eyes wide, his breath coming in short, sharp gasps, his thin, frail body trembling. He took another shaky step forward, his hands shaking, his eyes wide.

"Because I was there," he whispered, his voice low, trembling, his eyes wide, his hands trembling. "I was there when it happened. I was there when he... when he killed her."

Grace felt her heart stop, her breath catching in her throat, her mind going blank. She stared at Wallace, her eyes wide, her pulse racing, her mind spinning.

"What... what are you talking about?" she whispered, her voice shaking, her eyes wide, her heart pounding in her chest.

Wallace's eyes flicked nervously up and down the empty alley, his breath coming in short, sharp gasps, his thin, frail body trembling. He took another shaky step forward, his hands shaking, his eyes wide.

"I was there," he whispered, his voice low, trembling, his eyes wide, his hands trembling. "I saw him do it. I saw him kill her. And I've been covering it up ever since."

CHAPTER 22

The Confrontation

Grace's world felt like it was spiraling out of control. She stumbled back into the safety of her car, her fingers fumbling with the keys, her breaths coming in short, ragged gasps. The engine roared to life, the vibration beneath her hands a stark contrast to the numbness spreading through her body.

As she pulled away from the dark, narrow alley where she'd just faced Dr. Wallace, his words echoed in her mind, replaying over and over like a broken record.

"I was there. I saw him do it. I saw him kill her."

The city lights blurred past her as she sped through the rain-slicked streets, her mind racing, her pulse thundering in her ears. She felt the cold sweat trickling down her spine, the bitter taste of fear lingering in her mouth.

But as the initial shock wore off, a different feeling began to creep in – anger. A deep, burning rage that seemed to ignite every nerve ending in her body. She gripped the steering wheel tighter, her knuckles turning white, her jaw clenched, her heart pounding with a newfound fury.

How dare he? How dare Wallace try to poison her mind, try to twist her reality, try to turn her against her husband?

But then the doubt crept back in, seeping into her thoughts like a slow, insidious poison. What if he was telling the truth? What if David wasn't the man she thought he was? What if the man she'd shared her life with, the father of her children, the man who had once been her everything, was capable of something so... so monstrous?

Grace pulled into their driveway, her headlights cutting through the thick fog that had settled over the street, casting long, twisted shadows against the house. She killed the engine and sat there for a moment, her hands trembling on the steering wheel, her breath coming in short, shallow gasps.

The house loomed before her, dark and silent, its windows like empty, watchful eyes. She could see the faint glow of the living room light spilling out onto the front porch, a small beacon of warmth in the otherwise cold, damp night.

She stepped out of the car, her boots crunching against the gravel, the cold night air biting into her skin. She reached for the front door, her fingers trembling as she fumbled with the keys, her mind a chaotic whirlwind of fear, anger, and confusion.

The door creaked open, the warm, familiar scent of home washing over her, the faint sound of the television murmuring from the living room. She stepped inside, her heart pounding, her breath coming in short, shallow gasps, her pulse racing.

"David?" she called out, her voice shaking, her heart hammering in her chest. "David, are you home?"

There was a moment of silence, a long, pregnant pause that seemed to stretch on forever, the air around her thick with tension, the shadows deepening, closing in on her.

Then, she heard it – the soft, steady thud of footsteps coming down the stairs, the slow, deliberate creak of the old wooden steps as David made his way down to meet her.

He appeared at the top of the stairs, his silhouette framed against the warm, golden glow of the hallway light, his face cast in shadow, his eyes hidden in the darkness.

"Grace?" he said, his voice low, steady, his tone tinged with a faint note of concern. "Is everything okay? You're home late."

Grace felt a fresh wave of nausea rise in her throat, her heart pounding in her chest, her mind racing. She took a shaky step back, her fingers tightening around the strap of her purse, her breath coming in short, shallow gasps.

"I... I ran into Dr. Wallace tonight," she stammered, her voice trembling, her eyes wide, her heart racing. "He... he said some things, David. Some... some crazy, terrifying things."

David paused on the last step, his hand gripping the banister, his jaw tightening, his eyes narrowing slightly in the dim light.

"Wallace?" he said, his voice low, measured, his eyes dark, his jaw clenched. "What did he say?"

Grace swallowed hard, her heart pounding, her pulse racing, her mind spinning. She felt the walls closing in on her, the air growing thick, suffocating, her world tilting on its axis.

"He... he said you killed someone," she whispered, her voice shaking, her eyes wide, her heart racing. "He said he was there when it happened. That he's been covering it up ever since."

David froze, his body tensing, his jaw tightening, his eyes narrowing, a muscle in his jaw twitching. For a long, terrifying moment, he said nothing, the silence stretching between them like a taut, fraying wire, ready to snap at any moment.

Then, he took a slow, deliberate step down, his dark eyes locked on hers, his face expressionless, his jaw clenched, his fists tightening at his sides.

"And you believed him?" he said, his voice low, dangerous, his eyes cold, his jaw clenched, his body coiled like a spring, ready to strike.

Grace felt a fresh wave of fear wash over her, her heart pounding in her chest, her mind spinning, her pulse racing. She took a shaky step back, her back pressing against the cold, hard wall behind her, her breath coming in short, shallow gasps.

"I... I don't know what to believe," she whispered, her voice shaking, her eyes wide, her heart racing. "I don't know what's real anymore."

David's eyes darkened, his jaw tightening, his fists clenching at his sides, his body trembling with barely restrained rage. He took another slow, deliberate step forward, his dark eyes burning into hers, his breath coming in short, sharp gasps.

"You should have more faith in your husband, Grace," he whispered, his voice low, dangerous, his eyes cold, his jaw clenched. "Because if you start believing the lies of a madman, you'll lose everything."

Grace felt her heart stop, her breath catching in her throat, her mind going blank. She stared at him, her eyes wide, her pulse racing, her mind spinning.

David took another slow, deliberate step forward, his dark eyes locked on hers, his jaw clenched, his fists tightening at his sides. "And believe me, Grace," he whispered, his voice low, dangerous, his eyes cold, his jaw clenched. "You don't want to know what happens when you cross me."

Grace couldn't sleep. The confrontation with David had left her shaken, her mind a twisted mess of fear, confusion, and disbelief. She lay in bed, her body curled up beneath the heavy duvet, her eyes wide open, staring into the darkness, her heart racing, her mind spinning.

David's words echoed in her head, his cold, dangerous tone replaying over and over, each word a fresh stab of fear.

"Because if you start believing the lies of a madman, you'll lose everything."

She had never seen him like that before – so cold, so calculated, so... dangerous. It was like a stranger had stepped into their home, a dark, twisted reflection of the man she had loved for years, the father of her children, the man she had once trusted with her life.

But as the minutes ticked by, the darkness pressing in around her, a new thought crept into her mind, seeping into her consciousness like a slow, insidious poison.

What if David had been hiding this side of himself all along? What if this darkness had always been there, lurking beneath the surface, hidden behind his charming smile and loving words, his warm, reassuring touch?

Grace shivered, pulling the duvet up to her chin, her heart pounding, her breath coming in short, shallow gasps, her pulse racing. She felt the cold, sharp claws of fear tightening around her heart, the air around her growing thick, suffocating, her world tilting on its axis.

Unable to lie still any longer, she threw back the covers and slipped out of bed, her bare feet touching the cold, polished wooden floor, the chill biting into her skin, sending a shiver down her spine. She crept to the door, her heart racing, her breath coming in short, shallow gasps, her mind spinning.

She paused at the doorway, her hand trembling on the brass doorknob, her heart pounding, her pulse racing. She glanced back at the bed, at the dark, still figure of her husband lying beside her, his broad shoulders rising and falling with each slow, steady breath, his face hidden in the shadows.

For a moment, she considered waking him, confronting him again, demanding the truth, forcing him to reveal his secrets, to admit to the darkness she had seen in his eyes, the cold, calculated anger in his voice.

But then she remembered the way he had looked at her, the way his eyes had darkened, his jaw had tightened, his fists had clenched at his sides, his body trembling with barely restrained rage.

No. Not now. Not yet.

Instead, she slipped out of the bedroom, pulling the door closed behind her with a soft, muffled click, her heart racing, her breath coming in short, shallow gasps, her mind spinning. She padded down the hallway, her bare feet whispering against the cold, polished wooden floor, her pulse thundering in her ears, her mind a chaotic whirlwind of fear, anger, and confusion.

As she reached the bottom of the stairs, she paused, her hand gripping the polished wooden banister, her heart pounding, her pulse racing, her breath coming in short, shallow gasps. She glanced over her shoulder, half-expecting to see David standing at the top of the stairs, his dark eyes burning into hers, his jaw clenched, his fists tightening at his sides.

But the hallway was empty, the shadows deep and still, the air thick with tension, the silence oppressive, suffocating.

She stepped into the living room, her eyes adjusting to the darkness, the faint, ghostly glow of the streetlights outside casting long, twisted shadows against the walls. She crossed the room, her feet whispering against the cold, polished wooden floor, her heart pounding, her pulse racing, her mind spinning.

She reached the small wooden cabinet in the corner of the room, the one David had always kept locked, the one he had always been so protective of, the one he had forbidden her from touching, from even looking at.

Her fingers trembled as she reached for the small brass key hidden behind the family photo on the mantelpiece, her heart racing, her breath coming in short, shallow gasps, her mind spinning. She slipped the key into the lock, her fingers shaking, her pulse thundering in her ears, her breath catching in her throat.

The lock clicked open with a soft, metallic sound, the cabinet door creaking as she pulled it open, the darkness inside spilling out into the room, the air around her growing thick, suffocating, her world tilting on its axis.

She reached inside, her fingers brushing against the cold, smooth surface of a small, leather-bound journal, the pages thick and heavy, the cover worn and cracked, the edges frayed, the faint, musty scent of old paper filling her nostrils.

She pulled the journal out, her heart racing, her breath coming in short, shallow gasps, her pulse thundering in her ears, her mind spinning. She opened it to the first page, her eyes widening as she read the neat, precise handwriting scrawled across the yellowed paper, the ink dark and bold, the words sharp and cutting.

"To my dearest Grace," the first line read, the words a twisted mockery of the love letters he had once written to her, the sweet, heartfelt notes he had slipped into her purse, the tender, whispered words he had spoken into her ear late at night, his breath warm against her skin.

But as she read on, her heart pounding, her pulse racing, her breath coming in short, shallow gasps, her mind spinning, she realized that this was no love letter. This was a confession, a chilling, twisted account of his darkest thoughts, his deepest fears, his most terrifying secrets.

And as she reached the final page, her hands trembling, her eyes wide, her heart pounding, her pulse racing, her breath coming in short, shallow gasps, her mind spinning, she felt the ground shift beneath her, the air around her growing thick, suffocating, her world crumbling around her.

Because there, scrawled in David's neat, precise handwriting, were the words that would shatter her world, the words that would change everything, the words that would reveal the truth about the man she had once loved, the man she had once trusted, the man who had once been her everything.

"I killed her. And I would do it again."

Grace's hands trembled as she clutched the journal, the cold leather pressing into her palms, her heart pounding, her breath coming in short, ragged gasps, her pulse thundering in her ears. The words on the page blurred before her eyes, her mind spinning, her world crumbling around her.

"I killed her. And I would do it again."

The letters seemed to glow in the dim light, each stroke of ink a chilling reminder of the man she had once trusted, the man she had once loved, the father of her children, the man who now felt like a stranger, a ghost, a monster.

She stumbled back, her knees buckling, her back hitting the edge of the couch, the journal slipping from her grasp, falling to the floor with a dull, heavy thud, the pages fluttering open, the dark, twisted words spilling out into the room, filling the air around her with their chilling weight.

A sharp, icy wave of nausea crashed over her, her stomach twisting, her throat tightening, bile rising in her throat. She clapped a trembling hand over her mouth, her eyes wide, her breath coming in short, shallow gasps, her mind spinning.

Memories flooded her mind, flashing before her eyes like a twisted, broken film reel, the scenes playing out in sharp, jagged fragments, each one more horrifying than the last.

She remembered the first time she had met David, his charming smile, his warm, reassuring voice, his strong, protective arms wrapped around her, his dark, piercing eyes staring into hers, his lips brushing against her ear as he whispered sweet, loving words, promises of forever, vows of undying love.

She remembered the way he had held her the night she had told him she was pregnant, his hands shaking, his eyes bright with tears, his lips trembling as he whispered, *"We're going to be a family, Grace. You, me, and our little one. I promise to protect you, to keep you safe, to love you forever."*

But now, those memories felt twisted, tainted, poisoned by the truth she had just uncovered, the dark, terrifying truth hidden within the pages of the journal lying at her feet, the truth that had shattered her world, that had torn her life apart.

She took a deep, shuddering breath, her chest heaving, her pulse racing, her mind spinning, the air around her growing thick, suffocating, the darkness pressing in around her, her world crumbling beneath her feet.

And then, suddenly, a sharp, chilling realization cut through the fog of her fear, a cold, hard truth that sent a fresh wave of terror crashing over her, her heart pounding, her breath coming in short, shallow gasps, her pulse thundering in her ears.

The journal wasn't just a confession. It was a warning.

David had killed before. And if he felt threatened, if he felt cornered, if he felt that his secrets were about to be exposed, he could do it again.

And she was the only one who knew the truth.

Flashback – The First Lie

The summer of 2008. Grace had been six months pregnant with their first child, Emma. They had just moved into their new home, the small, charming two-story house on Maple Street, the one with the white picket fence, the rose bushes lining the front porch, the tall, swaying oak tree in the front yard.

It had been a warm, sunny afternoon, the air thick with the sweet, heady scent of freshly cut grass and blooming flowers, the sound of birdsong filling the air, the bright, golden sunlight streaming through the open windows, casting long, dancing shadows across the polished wooden floor.

Grace had been in the kitchen, her swollen belly brushing against the edge of the counter as she chopped vegetables for dinner, her mind drifting, her thoughts wandering, her heart swelling with love and anticipation, her pulse racing with excitement.

And then the phone had rung, the sharp, shrill sound cutting through the peaceful, sunlit silence, sending a jolt of fear racing down her spine, her heart pounding, her breath catching in her throat, her pulse thundering in her ears.

She had picked up the phone, her hands trembling, her breath coming in short, shallow gasps, her mind spinning, her pulse racing, the air around her growing thick, suffocating, the darkness pressing in around her, her world tilting on its axis.

It had been a woman's voice on the other end, soft, hesitant, her words slurred, her tone tinged with fear, desperation, panic.

"Is this Grace? Grace Thompson?"

Grace had frowned, her heart pounding, her pulse racing, her breath coming in short, shallow gasps, her mind spinning.

"Yes. Who is this?"

There had been a long, heavy pause on the other end of the line, the silence stretching out between them, thick, suffocating, oppressive.

And then, the woman had whispered, her voice trembling, her breath coming in short, shallow gasps, her words sharp, cutting, terrifying.

"Stay away from him. He's not who you think he is. He's dangerous. He's a liar. A killer."

Grace had stumbled back, her knees buckling, her back hitting the edge of the counter, the phone slipping from her grasp, clattering to the floor with a sharp, metallic crash, the woman's chilling words echoing in her mind, her heart pounding, her breath coming in short, shallow gasps, her pulse thundering in her ears, her mind spinning, her world crumbling around her.

David had walked in just as she picked up the phone, his dark, piercing eyes narrowing as he took in the sight of her pale, trembling form, his jaw tightening, his fists clenching at his sides, his body tensing, his breath coming in short, shallow gasps, his pulse racing.

"Grace, what's wrong?"

She had looked up at him, her eyes wide, her breath coming in short, shallow gasps, her mind spinning, her pulse racing, the air around her growing thick, suffocating, the darkness pressing in around her, her world tilting on its axis.

"Who was that woman, David?"

For a moment, he had frozen, his eyes widening, his jaw tightening, his fists clenching at his sides, his breath coming in short, shallow gasps, his pulse racing, his mind spinning, the air around him growing thick, suffocating, the darkness pressing in around him, his world tilting on its axis.

And then, he had forced a smile, his eyes dark, his voice cold, his words sharp, cutting, calculated.

"Just a wrong number, Grace. Just a wrong number."

But as he had wrapped his arms around her, his hands gripping her shoulders, his breath warm against her ear, his lips brushing against her cheek, his voice whispering sweet, reassuring words, she had felt a cold, sharp chill race down her spine, her heart pounding, her breath coming in short, shallow gasps, her pulse racing, her mind spinning.

And for the first time, she had felt a flicker of doubt, a whisper of fear, a shadow of suspicion, a tiny, insidious seed of mistrust that had taken root in her heart, slowly growing, spreading, twisting, poisoning her mind, her soul, her very being.

CHAPTER 23

The Web Tightens

The chill of early winter crept through the half-open window, sending a shiver down Grace's spine as she leaned against the cool kitchen counter, her fingers wrapped tightly around a steaming cup of tea. The distant hum of traffic outside, the soft rustle of leaves in the cold wind, the rhythmic ticking of the wall clock – all felt like a countdown to some inevitable disaster, a slow, steady march towards a revelation she was no longer sure she wanted.

David had left early that morning, his steps hurried, his movements tense, his eyes shadowed by the same darkness that had haunted him for weeks. She had watched him from the kitchen window as he climbed into his car, the engine roaring to life, the taillights glowing red like the eyes of a demon as he disappeared down the street, leaving her alone in the quiet, empty house.

Grace took a deep, shuddering breath, her fingers trembling as she took a sip of the scalding tea, the bitter liquid scorching her throat, the heat burning her tongue, the pain grounding her, anchoring her to the moment, the reality of her crumbling world.

Her mind drifted back to the journal she had found hidden in the false bottom of David's desk drawer, the dark, twisted words etched into the yellowed pages, the chilling confessions, the terrifying secrets, the damning evidence of the man she had married, the father of her children, the man she had once trusted, the man she had once loved.

She set the cup down on the counter with a sharp, metallic

clink, her heart pounding, her pulse racing, her breath coming in short, shallow gasps, the weight of her fear pressing down on her chest, suffocating her, drowning her in a sea of doubt, confusion, terror.

She needed answers. She needed the truth.

And there was only one person in the entire neighborhood who might know more than she let on, the one person who had always been watching, always been listening, always been lurking in the shadows, her sharp, beady eyes peering through the curtains, her thin, pale face pressed against the glass, her breath fogging up the window as she spied on the lives of her unsuspecting neighbors.

Mrs. Whitmore.

The creaking of the old, rusted hinges echoed down the narrow, dimly lit hallway as Grace pushed open the heavy, wooden door of Mrs. Whitmore's house, the musty, stale air rushing out to greet her, the faint, sickly sweet scent of decaying flowers and old, dusty books filling her nostrils, making her stomach turn, her skin crawl, her pulse quicken.

She stepped inside, the worn, threadbare carpet soft beneath her feet, the shadows stretching across the walls like twisted, grasping fingers, the flickering, yellow light from the old, cracked lamps casting long, dancing shapes on the faded wallpaper, the dark, swirling patterns moving, shifting, twisting in the corner of her eyes, like ghosts, like whispers, like echoes of the past.

"Grace, my dear," Mrs. Whitmore's voice drifted out from the shadowed depths of the living room, the words slow, drawn out, tinged with the faint, metallic edge of a poorly hidden smile, the sound sending a sharp, cold chill racing down Grace's spine, her heart pounding, her breath catching in her throat.

She stepped into the small, cluttered room, her eyes adjusting to the dim light, her pulse racing, her hands trembling as she took in the sight of the frail, thin, pale woman sitting in the high-backed, velvet armchair by the window, her thin, bony fingers curled around the worn, leather-bound book in her lap, her sharp, beady eyes gleaming behind her thick, wire-rimmed glasses, her thin, pale lips twisted into a crooked, knowing smile. "Please, sit," Mrs. Whitmore gestured to the small, rickety wooden chair across from her, the thin, cracked cushion sagging under its own weight, the dark, polished wood glinting in the dim light, the sharp, splintered edges catching the flickering, yellow glow.

Grace hesitated, her heart pounding, her breath coming in short, shallow gasps, her pulse thundering in her ears, her mind spinning, the air around her growing thick, suffocating, the darkness pressing in around her, her world tilting on its axis.

But she forced herself to move, to take a step forward, to cross the small, cluttered room, to lower herself into the fragile, creaking chair, the wooden legs groaning beneath her weight, the thin cushion sinking, the sharp, splintered edges pressing into the backs of her thighs, the discomfort grounding her, anchoring her to the moment, the reality of her crumbling world.

Mrs. Whitmore leaned forward, her thin, bony fingers tapping rhythmically against the leather cover of the book in her lap, her sharp, beady eyes never leaving Grace's face, her thin, pale lips twitching with barely contained amusement, her breath coming in short, shallow puffs, her pulse quickening, her mind spinning, the air around her growing thick, suffocating, the darkness pressing in around her, her world tilting on its axis.

"I've been expecting you, Grace," she whispered, her voice low, sharp, cutting, each word a dagger to Grace's heart, a cold, sharp blade twisting in her chest, her breath catching in her throat, her pulse racing, her mind spinning, the air around her growing thick, suffocating, the darkness pressing in around her, her world crumbling beneath her feet.

Grace's blood ran cold, her heart skipping a beat, her pulse racing, her breath coming in short, shallow gasps, her mind spinning, the air around her growing thick, suffocating, the darkness pressing in around her, her world tilting on its axis.

"How... how did you know?" Grace whispered, her voice

trembling, her words shaky, her breath catching in her throat, her pulse racing, her mind spinning, the air around her growing thick, suffocating, the darkness pressing in around her, her world crumbling beneath her feet.

Mrs. Whitmore's smile widened, her thin, pale lips stretching into a crooked, twisted grin, her sharp, beady eyes gleaming behind her thick, wire-rimmed glasses, her thin, bony fingers tapping rhythmically against the leather cover of the book in her lap, her breath coming in short, shallow puffs, her pulse quickening, her mind spinning, the air around her growing thick, suffocating, the darkness pressing in around her, her world tilting on its axis.

"Because, my dear," she whispered, her voice low, sharp, cutting, each word a dagger to Grace's heart, a cold, sharp blade twisting in her chest, her breath catching in her throat, her pulse racing, her mind spinning, the air around her growing thick, suffocating, the darkness pressing in around her, her world crumbling beneath her feet.

"I've been watching you. I've been watching all of you. And I know everything."

The air in Mrs. Whitmore's living room felt thick and heavy, clinging to Grace's skin like wet wool. Dust motes danced in the thin shafts of weak, gray light streaming through the dirty, lace curtains, the tiny particles swirling, spinning, floating in the still, stagnant air, like the ghosts of forgotten whispers, the echoes of long-dead secrets.

Grace gripped the edge of the rickety wooden chair, her knuckles white, her breath coming in short, shallow gasps, her heart pounding, her mind spinning, the air around her growing thick, suffocating, the darkness pressing in around her, her world tilting on its axis.

Mrs. Whitmore's sharp, beady eyes never left Grace's face, the thin, pale lips twisted into a crooked, knowing smile, her thin, bony fingers tapping rhythmically against the worn, leather-bound book in her lap, each tap a cold, sharp blade twisting in Grace's chest, each tap a dagger to her heart, each tap a reminder of the dark, twisted secrets hidden in the shadows, the secrets Grace was only just beginning to uncover.

"I've been watching you, Grace," Mrs. Whitmore whispered, her voice low, sharp, cutting, each word a dagger to Grace's heart, a cold, sharp blade twisting in her chest, her breath catching in her throat, her pulse racing, her mind spinning, the air around her growing thick, suffocating, the darkness pressing in around her, her world crumbling beneath her feet.

"Watching... me?" Grace stammered, her voice trembling, her words shaky, her breath catching in her throat, her pulse racing, her mind spinning, the air around her growing thick, suffocating, the darkness pressing in around her, her world tilting on its axis.

Mrs. Whitmore leaned back in her chair, the old, velvet upholstery groaning beneath her thin, bony frame, the leather-bound book in her lap creaking as she ran her thin, bony fingers over the cracked, brittle spine, her sharp, beady eyes never leaving Grace's face, her thin, pale lips twitching with barely contained amusement, her breath coming in short, shallow puffs, her pulse quickening, her mind spinning, the air around her growing thick, suffocating, the darkness pressing in around her, her world tilting on its axis.

"Oh, yes," she whispered, her voice low, sharp, cutting, each word a dagger to Grace's heart, a cold, sharp blade twisting in her chest, her breath catching in her throat, her pulse racing, her mind spinning, the air around her growing thick, suffocating, the darkness pressing in around her, her world crumbling beneath her feet.

"I know all about you, Grace. I know about David. I know about the lies, the secrets, the whispers in the dark. I know about the shadows lurking in the corners of your perfect little world."

Grace felt the blood drain from her face, her heart skipping a beat, her pulse racing, her breath coming in short, shallow gasps, her mind spinning, the air around her growing thick, suffocating, the darkness pressing in around her, her world crumbling beneath her feet.

"I... I don't understand," Grace whispered, her voice trembling, her words shaky, her breath catching in her throat, her pulse racing, her mind spinning, the air around her growing thick, suffocating, the darkness pressing in around her, her world tilting on its axis.

Mrs. Whitmore's smile widened, her thin, pale lips stretching into a crooked, twisted grin, her sharp, beady eyes gleaming behind her thick, wire-rimmed glasses, her thin, bony fingers tapping rhythmically against the leather cover of the book in her lap, her breath coming in short, shallow puffs, her pulse quickening, her mind spinning, the air around her growing thick, suffocating, the darkness pressing in around her, her world tilting on its axis.

"Of course you don't," she whispered, her voice low, sharp, cutting, each word a dagger to Grace's heart, a cold, sharp blade twisting in her chest, her breath catching in her throat, her pulse racing, her mind spinning, the air around her growing thick, suffocating, the darkness pressing in around her, her world crumbling beneath her feet.

"You see, Grace, you're not the first woman David has deceived. You're not the first wife he's lied to, the first family he's destroyed, the first life he's shattered."

Grace's blood ran cold, her heart skipping a beat, her pulse racing, her breath coming in short, shallow gasps, her mind spinning, the air around her growing thick, suffocating, the darkness pressing in around her, her world tilting on its axis.

"What... what are you talking about?" Grace stammered, her voice trembling, her words shaky, her breath catching in her throat, her pulse racing, her mind spinning, the air around her growing thick, suffocating, the darkness pressing in around her, her world crumbling beneath her feet.

Mrs. Whitmore leaned forward, her thin, bony fingers gripping the edges of the leather-bound book in her lap, her sharp, beady eyes gleaming behind her thick, wire-rimmed glasses, her thin, pale lips twisted into a crooked, twisted grin, her breath coming in short, shallow puffs, her pulse quickening, her mind spinning, the air around her growing thick, suffocating, the darkness pressing in around her, her world tilting on its axis.

"Because, my dear," she whispered, her voice low, sharp, cutting, each word a dagger to Grace's heart, a cold, sharp blade twisting in her chest, her breath catching in her throat, her pulse racing, her mind spinning, the air around her growing thick, suffocating, the darkness pressing in around her, her world crumbling beneath her feet.

"I was his first."

The words echoed in Grace's mind, bouncing off the walls of her thoughts like a ricocheting bullet.

"I was his first."

She blinked, trying to make sense of the sentence, but it felt like trying to solve a puzzle with pieces that didn't fit. She swallowed, her throat dry, her tongue thick, her heart thundering in her chest.

Mrs. Whitmore leaned back, her thin, bony fingers interlaced, the leather-bound book still in her lap, her sharp, beady eyes never leaving Grace's face, her thin, pale lips twisted into that same crooked, twisted grin, her breath coming in short, shallow puffs, her pulse quickening, her mind spinning, the air around her growing thick, suffocating, the darkness pressing in around her, her world tilting on its axis.

Grace opened her mouth to speak, but no words came out. She felt like the walls were closing in on her, the shadows creeping closer, the darkness swallowing her whole.

Mrs. Whitmore let out a dry, brittle laugh, the sound like the rustling of dead leaves in the wind, like the creaking of old, rotting wood, like the whisper of death itself.

"Oh, don't look so surprised, my dear," she said, her voice low, sharp, cutting, each word a dagger to Grace's heart, a cold, sharp blade twisting in her chest, her breath catching in her throat, her pulse racing, her mind spinning, the air around her growing thick, suffocating, the darkness pressing in around her, her world crumbling beneath her feet.

"David was a different man back then," Mrs. Whitmore

continued, her sharp, beady eyes gleaming behind her thick, wire-rimmed glasses, her thin, bony fingers tapping rhythmically against the leather cover of the book in her lap, her breath coming in short, shallow puffs, her pulse quickening, her mind spinning, the air around her growing thick, suffocating, the darkness pressing in around her, her world tilting on its axis. "A reckless, ambitious, dangerous man. The kind of man who took what he wanted, who destroyed anything that got in his way, who lied, cheated, manipulated, and broke hearts without a second thought."

Grace felt a chill run down her spine, her blood running cold, her heart skipping a beat, her pulse racing, her breath coming in short, shallow gasps, her mind spinning, the air around her growing thick, suffocating, the darkness pressing in around her, her world crumbling beneath her feet.

"What... what do you mean?" Grace whispered, her voice trembling, her words shaky, her breath catching in her throat, her pulse racing, her mind spinning, the air around her growing thick, suffocating, the darkness pressing in around her, her world tilting on its axis.

Mrs. Whitmore leaned forward, her thin, bony fingers gripping the edges of the leather-bound book in her lap, her sharp, beady eyes gleaming behind her thick, wire-rimmed glasses, her thin, pale lips twisted into a crooked, twisted grin, her breath coming in short, shallow puffs, her pulse quickening, her mind spinning, the air around her growing thick, suffocating, the darkness pressing in around her, her world tilting on its axis.

"I was young once, Grace," she whispered, her voice low, sharp, cutting, each word a dagger to Grace's heart, a cold, sharp blade twisting in her chest, her breath catching in her throat, her pulse racing, her mind spinning, the air around her growing thick, suffocating, the darkness pressing in around her, her world crumbling beneath her feet.

"I was beautiful, desirable, full of life and passion and fire. I was the woman who made David who he is today. I was the one who taught him the art of deception, the one who molded him into the master manipulator he is today, the one who taught him how to lie, how to cheat, how to destroy."

Grace felt her knees go weak, her legs trembling, her heart pounding, her breath coming in short, shallow gasps, her mind spinning, the air around her growing thick, suffocating, the darkness pressing in around her, her world crumbling beneath her feet.

"No..." Grace whispered, her voice trembling, her words shaky, her breath catching in her throat, her pulse racing, her mind spinning, the air around her growing thick, suffocating, the darkness pressing in around her, her world tilting on its axis.

"Oh, yes," Mrs. Whitmore whispered, her thin, bony fingers tightening around the edges of the leather-bound book in her lap, her sharp, beady eyes gleaming behind her thick, wire-rimmed glasses, her thin, pale lips twisted into a crooked, twisted grin, her breath coming in short, shallow puffs, her pulse quickening, her mind spinning, the air around her growing thick, suffocating, the darkness pressing in around her, her world tilting on its axis.

"I was his first. His first love. His first lie. His first betrayal. His first broken heart. His first destroyed life."

Grace felt the world spin around her, the ground tilting beneath her feet, the air growing thick, suffocating, the darkness pressing in around her, her world crumbling beneath her feet, her heart shattering into a million pieces, her mind spinning, her soul breaking, the shadows closing in around her, the darkness swallowing her whole.

Mrs. Whitmore leaned back, her thin, bony fingers interlaced, the leather-bound book still in her lap, her sharp, beady eyes never leaving Grace's face, her thin, pale lips twisted into that same crooked, twisted grin, her breath coming in short, shallow puffs, her pulse quickening, her mind spinning, the air around her growing thick, suffocating, the darkness pressing in around her, her world tilting on its axis.

"And now, my dear," she whispered, her voice low, sharp, cutting, each word a dagger to Grace's heart, a cold, sharp blade twisting in her chest, her breath catching in her throat, her pulse racing, her mind spinning, the air around her growing thick, suffocating, the darkness pressing in around her, her world crumbling beneath her feet.

"It's your turn."

CHAPTER 24

The Puppet Master

G race staggered back, her hand gripping the edge of the kitchen counter for support. Mrs. Whitmore's words hung in the air, sharp and cold, slicing through the fragile peace Grace had clung to. Her breath came in short, sharp gasps, her heart thundering in her chest, her mind spinning as if the ground beneath her had vanished.

The creaking of Mrs. Whitmore's old leather chair echoed through the room as the old woman leaned back, her eyes never leaving Grace's face, her fingers still clutching the edges of the leather-bound book in her lap.

"I can see it in your eyes, Grace," she whispered, her voice low, sharp, cutting, each word a dagger to Grace's heart, a cold, sharp blade twisting in her chest. "You're shocked, confused, angry. But most of all, you're scared."

Grace felt the air grow thick, suffocating, the darkness pressing in around her, the shadows closing in, her world crumbling beneath her feet. She forced herself to stand tall, to breathe, to push back the fear, the doubt, the rising panic. She needed answers, and she needed them now.

"Why are you telling me this?" Grace demanded, her voice trembling, her words shaky, her breath coming in short, shallow gasps, her pulse racing, her mind spinning, the air around her growing thick, suffocating, the darkness pressing in around her, her world tilting on its axis.

Mrs. Whitmore's thin, pale lips twisted into a crooked, twisted grin, her sharp, beady eyes gleaming behind her thick, wire-rimmed glasses, her thin, bony fingers tapping rhythmically against the leather cover of the book in her lap.

"Because, my dear," she whispered, leaning forward, her eyes narrowing, her breath coming in short, shallow puffs, her pulse quickening, her mind spinning, the air around her growing thick, suffocating, the darkness pressing in around her, her world tilting on its axis.

"I need you to understand something very important."

Grace swallowed, her throat dry, her tongue thick, her heart thundering in her chest, her pulse racing, her mind spinning, the air around her growing thick, suffocating, the darkness pressing in around her, her world crumbling beneath her feet.

"What... what do you mean?" Grace whispered, her voice trembling, her words shaky, her breath catching in her throat, her pulse racing, her mind spinning, the air around her growing thick, suffocating, the darkness pressing in around her, her world tilting on its axis.

Mrs. Whitmore leaned back, her thin, bony fingers interlaced, the leather-bound book still in her lap, her sharp, beady eyes never leaving Grace's face, her thin, pale lips twisted into that same crooked, twisted grin, her breath coming in short, shallow puffs, her pulse quickening, her mind spinning, the air around her growing thick, suffocating, the darkness pressing in around her, her world tilting on its axis.

"I am the reason you met David," she whispered, her voice low, sharp, cutting, each word a dagger to Grace's heart, a cold, sharp blade twisting in her chest, her breath catching in her throat, her pulse racing, her mind spinning, the air around her growing thick, suffocating, the darkness pressing in around her, her world crumbling beneath her feet.

Grace felt the world spin around her, the ground tilting beneath her feet, the air growing thick, suffocating, the darkness pressing in around her, her world crumbling beneath her feet, her heart shattering into a million pieces, her mind spinning, her soul breaking, the shadows closing in around her, the darkness swallowing her whole.

"What... what are you talking about?" Grace whispered, her

voice trembling, her words shaky, her breath catching in her throat, her pulse racing, her mind spinning, the air around her growing thick, suffocating, the darkness pressing in around her, her world tilting on its axis.

Mrs. Whitmore's twisted grin widened, her sharp, beady eyes gleaming behind her thick, wire-rimmed glasses, her thin, bony fingers tightening around the edges of the leather-bound book in her lap, her breath coming in short, shallow puffs, her pulse quickening, her mind spinning, the air around her growing thick, suffocating, the darkness pressing in around her, her world tilting on its axis.

"I'm the one who introduced you to David," she whispered, her voice low, sharp, cutting, each word a dagger to Grace's heart, a cold, sharp blade twisting in her chest, her breath catching in her throat, her pulse racing, her mind spinning, the air around her growing thick, suffocating, the darkness pressing in around her, her world crumbling beneath her feet.

"I'm the one who planted the seeds, who pulled the strings, who set the stage, who orchestrated every moment of your relationship, who guided every step of your journey, who controlled every aspect of your life."

Grace felt her knees go weak, her legs trembling, her heart pounding, her breath coming in short, shallow gasps, her mind spinning, the air around her growing thick, suffocating, the darkness pressing in around her, her world crumbling beneath her feet.

"No..." Grace whispered, her voice trembling, her words shaky, her breath catching in her throat, her pulse racing, her mind spinning, the air around her growing thick, suffocating, the darkness pressing in around her, her world tilting on its axis.

"Oh, yes," Mrs. Whitmore whispered, her thin, bony fingers tightening around the edges of the leather-bound book in her lap, her sharp, beady eyes gleaming behind her thick, wire-rimmed glasses, her thin, pale lips twisted into a crooked, twisted grin, her breath coming in short, shallow puffs, her pulse quickening, her mind spinning, the air around her growing thick, suffocating, the darkness pressing in around her, her world tilting on its axis.

"I'm the puppet master, my dear. I hold the strings. I control the game. I decide who wins and who loses, who lives and who dies, who loves and who suffers, who rises and who falls."

Grace felt the world spin around her, the ground tilting beneath her feet, the air growing thick, suffocating, the darkness pressing in around her, her world crumbling beneath her feet, her heart shattering into a million pieces, her mind spinning, her soul breaking, the shadows closing in around her, the darkness swallowing her whole.

The room fell into a tense silence, the air thick with unspoken words, the weight of hidden truths pressing down on them both. Grace felt her pulse thrumming in her ears, a steady, deafening beat that drowned out every rational thought. Mrs. Whitmore's eyes never wavered, cold and calculating, sharp as a blade, her twisted smile revealing nothing but a chilling sense of control.

Grace took a shaky step back, her mind racing, a thousand questions battling for dominance, each one more terrifying than the last.

"What... what do you mean you introduced us?" Grace whispered, her voice trembling, her fingers clutching the counter for support, her legs weak, her heart pounding, her mind spinning, the air around her growing thick, suffocating, the darkness pressing in around her, her world tilting on its axis.

Mrs. Whitmore chuckled, a low, guttural sound, her thin, bony fingers drumming rhythmically against the leather-bound book in her lap, her eyes never leaving Grace's face, her breath coming in short, shallow puffs, her pulse quickening, her mind spinning, the air around her growing thick, suffocating, the darkness pressing in around her, her world tilting on its axis.

"Oh, my dear," she whispered, leaning forward, her eyes narrowing, her breath coming in short, shallow puffs, her pulse quickening, her mind spinning, the air around her growing thick, suffocating, the darkness pressing in around her, her world tilting on its axis.

"I'm not just your nosy neighbor," she continued, her voice low, sharp, cutting, each word a dagger to Grace's heart, a cold, sharp blade twisting in her chest, her breath catching in her throat, her pulse racing, her mind spinning, the air around her growing thick, suffocating, the darkness pressing in around her, her world crumbling beneath her feet.

"I'm the one who brought David into your life. I'm the one who planted the seeds of your so-called love story. I'm the one who orchestrated every moment, every twist, every turn, every heartbreak."

Grace felt her knees buckle, her legs trembling, her heart pounding, her breath coming in short, shallow gasps, her mind spinning, the air around her growing thick, suffocating, the darkness pressing in around her, her world crumbling beneath her feet.

"Why?" Grace choked, her voice trembling, her words shaky, her breath catching in her throat, her pulse racing, her mind spinning, the air around her growing thick, suffocating, the darkness pressing in around her, her world tilting on its axis. "Why would you do that?"

Mrs. Whitmore's twisted grin widened, her sharp, beady eyes gleaming behind her thick, wire-rimmed glasses, her thin, bony fingers tightening around the edges of the leather-bound book in her lap, her breath coming in short, shallow puffs, her pulse quickening, her mind spinning, the air around her growing thick, suffocating, the darkness pressing in around her, her world tilting on its axis.

"Because, my dear," she whispered, her voice low, sharp, cutting, each word a dagger to Grace's heart, a cold, sharp blade twisting in her chest, her breath catching in her throat, her pulse racing, her mind spinning, the air around her growing thick, suffocating, the darkness pressing in around her, her world crumbling beneath her feet.

"I have a history with David... a history you know nothing about."

Grace's breath caught in her throat, her pulse racing, her mind spinning, the air around her growing thick, suffocating, the darkness pressing in around her, her world crumbling beneath her feet.

"What... what are you talking about?" Grace whispered, her voice trembling, her words shaky, her breath catching in her throat, her pulse racing, her mind spinning, the air around her growing thick, suffocating, the darkness pressing in around her, her world tilting on its axis.

Mrs. Whitmore leaned back, her thin, bony fingers tightening around the edges of the leather-bound book in her lap, her sharp, beady eyes never leaving Grace's face, her thin, pale lips twisted into that same crooked, twisted grin, her breath coming in short, shallow puffs, her pulse quickening, her mind spinning, the air around her growing thick, suffocating, the darkness pressing in around her, her world tilting on its axis.

"I knew David long before you ever met him, my dear. Long before you even knew his name. Long before you became his wife. Long before you became a part of his carefully constructed facade."

Grace felt her world tilt, her heart shatter, her mind spin, the air around her growing thick, suffocating, the darkness pressing in around her, her world crumbling beneath her feet.

"You see," Mrs. Whitmore continued, her voice low, sharp, cutting, each word a dagger to Grace's heart, a cold, sharp blade twisting in her chest, her breath catching in her throat, her pulse racing, her mind spinning, the air around her growing thick, suffocating, the darkness pressing in around her, her world crumbling beneath her feet.

"David and I have a history... a dark, twisted, complicated history. A history filled with secrets, lies, betrayals, and broken promises. A history that you know nothing about. A history that I have worked very, very hard to keep hidden from you."

Grace felt her knees buckle, her legs trembling, her heart pounding, her breath coming in short, shallow gasps, her mind spinning, the air around her growing thick, suffocating, the darkness pressing in around her, her world crumbling beneath her feet.

"What... what do you mean?" Grace choked, her voice trembling, her words shaky, her breath catching in her throat, her pulse racing, her mind spinning, the air around her growing thick, suffocating, the darkness pressing in around her, her world tilting on its axis.

Mrs. Whitmore's twisted grin widened, her sharp, beady eyes gleaming behind her thick, wire-rimmed glasses, her thin, bony fingers tightening around the edges of the leather-bound book in her lap, her breath coming in short, shallow puffs, her pulse quickening, her mind spinning, the air around her growing thick, suffocating, the darkness pressing in around her, her world tilting on its axis.

"I was his first wife, Grace. His first and only true love."

Grace felt her world shatter, her heart break, her mind spin, the air around her growing thick, suffocating, the darkness pressing in around her, her world crumbling beneath her feet, her soul breaking, the shadows closing in around her, the darkness swallowing her whole.

Grace staggered back a step, her mind reeling, her pulse thundering in her ears. Mrs. Whitmore's words echoed in her head, each one a cold, sharp blade twisting deeper into her chest. She clutched the back of the kitchen chair for support, her breath coming in short, panicked gasps, her fingers trembling, her heart pounding, her world tilting on its axis.

This couldn't be true. It couldn't. David had always been so honest, so loving, so perfect. The kind of husband every woman dreamed of. The kind of father every child deserved. How could he have hidden something like this from her? How could he have lied so effortlessly, so convincingly, for so long?

Mrs. Whitmore watched her with a twisted, almost satisfied smile, her sharp, beady eyes gleaming with a dark, malicious light, her thin, bony fingers tapping rhythmically against the leather cover of her book, her sharp, cracked nails clicking softly against the worn, cracked leather, each tap echoing like a death knell in the tense, suffocating silence of the kitchen.

Grace's mind raced, her pulse quickened, her heart pounded, the air around her growing thick, suffocating, the shadows closing in around her, her world crumbling beneath her feet. She felt a cold, sinking dread spread through her chest, a creeping, insidious fear that twisted her stomach into tight, painful knots, her breath catching in her throat, her mind spinning, the darkness pressing in around her.

"No," she whispered, her voice trembling, her words shaky, her breath catching in her throat, her pulse racing, her mind spinning, the air around her growing thick, suffocating, the darkness pressing in around her, her world crumbling beneath her feet. "You're lying. You have to be lying. David would never... he would never..."

"Oh, but he would," Mrs. Whitmore hissed, her voice low, sharp, cutting, each word a dagger to Grace's heart, a cold, sharp blade twisting in her chest, her breath catching in her throat, her pulse racing, her mind spinning, the air around her growing thick, suffocating, the darkness pressing in around her, her world crumbling beneath her feet. "And he has. For years. Decades, even. He's a master of deception, a skilled manipulator, a liar, a cheat, a thief. He has built his entire life on a foundation of lies, and you, my dear, are just another pawn in his twisted game."

Grace felt a cold, sinking dread spread through her chest, her breath coming in short, shallow gasps, her pulse racing, her mind spinning, the air around her growing thick, suffocating, the darkness pressing in around her, her world crumbling beneath her feet.

And then, like a sudden flash of lightning, a memory surfaced, a fleeting, half-forgotten moment from years ago, a whisper from the past that sent a cold, sharp shock of fear through her veins, her pulse quickening, her breath catching in her throat, her heart pounding, her mind spinning, the air around her growing thick, suffocating, the darkness pressing in around her.

It was a family gathering, years before she had met David, a sunny afternoon in the garden of her childhood home, her parents laughing, her siblings playing, the warm, golden sunlight filtering through the leaves of the old oak tree in the backyard, the sweet, heady scent of freshly cut grass filling the air, the sound of her father's deep, booming voice echoing through the garden, his hearty, infectious laughter ringing out over the gentle, rustling whispers of the wind.

She had been sitting on the porch steps, a glass of lemonade in her hand, her bare feet curled beneath her, her eyes closed, her face turned up to the warm, golden sunlight, her mind drifting, her thoughts wandering, the gentle, soothing warmth of the sun on her skin, the soft, rhythmic rustle of the leaves in the breeze, the distant, melodic chirping of the birds in the trees.

And then, out of nowhere, her father's voice had cut through the gentle, soothing peace of the afternoon, his tone low, sharp, tense, a cold, hard edge to his words that had sent a sudden, sharp jolt of fear through her chest, her pulse quickening, her breath catching in her throat, her heart pounding, her mind spinning, the air around her growing thick, suffocating, the darkness pressing in around her, her world crumbling beneath her feet.

"I don't want that man near my family," he had said, his voice low, sharp, cutting, his words dripping with anger, his jaw clenched, his fists balled at his sides, his eyes hard, dark, his entire body tense, rigid, his face twisted into a mask of cold, hard fury, his breath coming in short, harsh gasps, his pulse racing, his heart pounding, his mind spinning, the air around him growing thick, suffocating, the darkness pressing in around him, his world crumbling beneath his feet.

Grace had opened her eyes, her breath catching in her throat, her pulse quickening, her heart pounding, her mind spinning, the air around her growing thick, suffocating, the darkness pressing in around her, her world tilting on its axis, her mind struggling to process the sudden, jarring shift in the atmosphere, the cold, hard edge to her father's words, the sharp, biting tension in his voice, the dark, twisted anger in his eyes.

And then she had seen him.

A man standing in the shadows at the edge of the garden, his tall, lean figure half-hidden behind the thick, twisting branches of the old oak tree, his face obscured, his dark, piercing eyes glinting in the shadows, his jaw clenched, his fists balled at his sides, his entire body tense, rigid, his breath coming in short, harsh gasps, his pulse racing, his heart pounding, his mind spinning, the air around him growing thick, suffocating, the darkness pressing in around him, his world crumbling beneath his feet.

She had only seen him for a moment, a fleeting, half-forgotten glimpse, a shadow in the darkness, a ghost from the past, a whisper from a forgotten time, but the memory had stayed with her, a cold, sharp, twisting knot of fear in the pit of her stomach, a dark, twisted whisper at the back of her mind, a cold, hard lump in her throat, a sharp, stinging ache in her chest.

And now, standing in Mrs. Whitmore's dim, shadowed kitchen, the air thick, suffocating, the darkness pressing in around her, her world crumbling beneath her feet, Grace felt that same cold, sharp, twisting knot of fear tighten in her chest, her breath catching in her throat, her pulse racing, her heart pounding, her mind spinning, the air around her growing thick, suffocating, the darkness pressing in around her.

"Oh my God," she whispered, her voice trembling, her words shaky, her breath catching in her throat, her pulse racing, her mind spinning, the air around her growing thick, suffocating, the darkness pressing in around her. "It was him. It was David. My father was talking about David."

CHAPTER 25

Secrets in the Shadows

Grace stumbled back into her kitchen, her mind spinning, her heart racing, her breath coming in short, panicked gasps. She clutched the edge of the counter for support, her fingers trembling, her pulse thundering in her ears, her vision swimming, her thoughts a chaotic, tangled web of fear, anger, disbelief, and confusion.

How could she have been so blind? How could she have missed the signs? The whispers, the half-hidden glances, the cold, sharp edge to her father's voice all those years ago, the shadowed figure lurking at the edge of the garden, the ghost from her past, the man her father had warned her about, the man she had married, the father of her children, the love of her life.

David.

The thought of him, the mere whisper of his name, sent a cold, sharp jolt of fear through her chest, her pulse quickening, her breath catching in her throat, her heart pounding, her mind spinning, the air around her growing thick, suffocating, the darkness pressing in around her, her world crumbling beneath her feet.

How could she have been so blind?

She staggered to the sink, her fingers gripping the cold, hard edge of the porcelain, her breath coming in short, shallow gasps, her pulse racing, her heart pounding, her mind spinning, the air around her growing thick, suffocating, the darkness pressing in around her.

She splashed cold water on her face, the icy shock jolting her back to reality, her mind clearing, her pulse steadying, her breath evening out, her thoughts untangling, the chaos in her mind settling, the darkness receding, her world tilting back into focus.

She straightened, her fingers gripping the edge of the sink, her jaw clenched, her eyes hard, dark, her breath coming in slow, steady, controlled bursts, her pulse racing, her heart pounding, her mind spinning, the air around her growing thick, suffocating, the darkness pressing in around her.

She had to confront him. She had to know the truth.

David was in his study, the dim, flickering glow of his desk lamp casting long, twisted shadows across the walls, the soft, rhythmic ticking of the grandfather clock in the corner echoing through the tense, suffocating silence, his fingers drumming against the smooth, polished surface of his desk, his jaw clenched, his eyes dark, hard, his mind racing, his pulse quickening, his heart pounding, his breath coming in short, shallow gasps.

He had been expecting this. He had known this day would come, the day when his carefully constructed world would come crashing down around him, his secrets exposed, his lies unravelled, his past catching up with him, the shadows he had tried so hard to outrun closing in around him.

But he hadn't expected it to be today. Not like this.

The door creaked open, the soft, hesitant sound echoing through the tense, suffocating silence of the room, the shadows twisting, stretching, contorting, the darkness pressing in around him, his pulse quickening, his heart pounding, his breath catching in his throat, his mind spinning, the air around him growing thick, suffocating, the darkness pressing in around him, his world crumbling beneath his feet.

Grace stepped into the room, her bare feet whispering against the cold, hard wooden floor, her long, dark hair falling in loose, tangled waves around her face, her eyes wide, dark, her jaw clenched, her breath coming in short, shallow gasps, her pulse racing, her heart pounding, her mind spinning, the air around her growing thick, suffocating, the darkness pressing in around her, her world crumbling beneath her feet.

She closed the door behind her with a soft, final click, the sound echoing through the tense, suffocating silence of the room, her pulse quickening, her heart pounding, her breath catching in her throat, her mind spinning, the air around her growing thick, suffocating, the darkness pressing in around her, her world crumbling beneath her feet.

David looked up, his fingers stilling on the smooth, polished surface of his desk, his jaw clenched, his eyes dark, hard, his breath coming in short, shallow gasps, his pulse racing, his heart pounding, his mind spinning, the air around him growing thick, suffocating, the darkness pressing in around him, his world crumbling beneath his feet.

"Grace," he said, his voice low, sharp, tense, a cold, hard edge to his words, his jaw clenched, his eyes dark, hard, his breath coming in short, shallow gasps, his pulse racing, his heart pounding, his mind spinning, the air around him growing thick, suffocating, the darkness pressing in around him, his world crumbling beneath his feet.

She stared at him, her eyes hard, dark, her jaw clenched, her breath coming in short, shallow gasps, her pulse racing, her heart pounding, her mind spinning, the air around her growing thick, suffocating, the darkness pressing in around her, her world crumbling beneath her feet.

"Who are you?" she whispered, her voice trembling, her words shaky, her breath catching in her throat, her pulse racing, her heart pounding, her mind spinning, the air around her growing thick, suffocating, the darkness pressing in around her, her world crumbling beneath her feet.

David's jaw clenched, his fingers curling into tight, white-knuckled fists, his pulse racing, his heart pounding, his breath catching in his throat, his mind spinning, the air around him growing thick, suffocating, the darkness pressing in around him, his world crumbling beneath his feet.

"I'm your husband," he said, his voice low, sharp, tense, a cold, hard edge to his words, his jaw clenched, his eyes dark, hard, his breath coming in short, shallow gasps, his pulse racing, his heart pounding, his mind spinning, the air around him growing thick, suffocating, the darkness pressing in around him, his world crumbling beneath his feet.

"No," Grace said, her voice trembling, her words shaky, her breath catching in her throat, her pulse racing, her heart pounding, her mind spinning, the air around her growing thick, suffocating, the darkness pressing in around her, her world crumbling beneath her feet. "You're not. You're a stranger. A liar. A ghost. A shadow."

David's jaw clenched, his fingers tightening around the edge of his desk, his pulse racing, his heart pounding, his breath catching in his throat, his mind spinning, the air around him growing thick, suffocating, the darkness pressing in around him, his world crumbling beneath his feet.

And in that moment, he knew he had lost her.

Grace's mind raced as she replayed the conversation in the study over and over, her pulse still pounding, her breath coming in short, shallow bursts. She had confronted him, finally looked him in the eyes and demanded the truth, but all she got was cold, calculated deflection. The man she had married, the father of her children, the love of her life – a stranger, a ghost, a shadow.

Yet, there was something else in his eyes, a flicker of fear, a glint of desperation, a crack in his carefully constructed facade. She had seen it, felt it, the tremor in his voice, the tightness in his jaw, the way his fingers had curled into tight, white-knuckled fists as he met her gaze.

David was hiding something. Something big.

The next morning, Grace found herself standing at her kitchen window, staring out at the quiet, sun-drenched street, her mind spinning, her pulse quickening, her breath catching in her throat. She had barely slept, her thoughts racing, her heart pounding, the shadows of her doubts creeping in around her, the darkness pressing in on her mind, her world crumbling beneath her feet.

Mrs. Whitmore's house stood across the street, its windows

dark, its garden overgrown, its walls crumbling, the air around it thick, suffocating, the darkness pressing in around it.

Grace's jaw clenched, her fingers tightening around the edge of the counter, her breath coming in short, shallow gasps, her pulse racing, her heart pounding, her mind spinning, the air around her growing thick, suffocating, the darkness pressing in around her, her world crumbling beneath her feet.

She had always thought of Mrs. Whitmore as a harmless old busybody, a nosy neighbor with too much time on her hands, her prying eyes and sharp tongue more of a nuisance than a threat. But now, standing at her window, her mind racing, her pulse quickening, her breath catching in her throat, she felt a chill run down her spine, a cold, sharp jolt of fear, a gnawing, clawing, suffocating dread.

What if Mrs. Whitmore knew more than she let on? What if she had seen something, heard something, pieced together the puzzle pieces Grace had missed, the clues she had ignored, the whispers she had brushed aside?

Later that afternoon, Grace found herself standing at Mrs. Whitmore's door, her fingers curled into tight, white-knuckled fists, her pulse racing, her heart pounding, her breath coming in short, shallow gasps, her mind spinning, the air around her growing thick, suffocating, the darkness pressing in around her, her world crumbling beneath her feet.

She hesitated for a moment, her fingers trembling, her jaw clenched, her breath catching in her throat, her pulse quickening, her heart pounding, her mind spinning, the air around her growing thick, suffocating, the darkness pressing in around her, her world crumbling beneath her feet.

Then she knocked.

The door creaked open, the soft, hesitant sound echoing through the tense, suffocating silence of the hallway, the shadows twisting, stretching, contorting, the darkness pressing in around her, her pulse quickening, her heart pounding, her breath catching in her throat, her mind spinning, the air around her growing thick, suffocating, the darkness pressing in around her, her world crumbling beneath her feet.

Mrs. Whitmore's sharp, piercing eyes met hers, the old woman's thin, wrinkled face twisted into a tight, suspicious scowl, her bony fingers curled into tight, white-knuckled fists, her breath coming in short, shallow gasps, her pulse racing, her heart pounding, her mind spinning, the air around her growing thick, suffocating, the darkness pressing in around her, her world crumbling beneath her feet.

"Grace," Mrs. Whitmore said, her voice low, sharp, tense, a cold, hard edge to her words, her jaw clenched, her eyes dark, hard, her breath coming in short, shallow gasps, her pulse racing, her heart pounding, her mind spinning, the air around her growing thick, suffocating, the darkness pressing in around her, her world crumbling beneath her feet.

"I need to talk to you," Grace said, her voice trembling, her words shaky, her breath catching in her throat, her pulse racing, her heart pounding, her mind spinning, the air around her growing thick, suffocating, the darkness pressing in around her, her world crumbling beneath her feet.

Mrs. Whitmore stepped back, her thin, bony fingers tightening around the edge of the door, her jaw clenched, her eyes dark, hard, her breath coming in short, shallow gasps, her pulse racing, her heart pounding, her mind spinning, the air around her growing thick, suffocating, the darkness pressing in around her, her world crumbling beneath her feet.

"Come in," she said, her voice low, sharp, tense, a cold, hard edge to her words, her jaw clenched, her eyes dark, hard, her breath coming in short, shallow gasps, her pulse racing, her heart pounding, her mind spinning, the air around her growing thick, suffocating, the darkness pressing in around her, her world crumbling beneath her feet.

Grace stepped into the dark, shadowed hallway, her breath catching in her throat, her pulse racing, her heart pounding, her mind spinning, the air around her growing thick, suffocating, the darkness pressing in around her, her world crumbling beneath her feet.

She had no idea what she was about to uncover, but she could feel it, the shadows closing in around her, the darkness pressing in on her mind, her world crumbling beneath her feet.

Grace stepped into Mrs. Whitmore's musty living room, the air thick with the scent of old books, stale perfume, and faint traces of mothballs. The heavy curtains, drawn tightly against the afternoon sun, cast long, twisted shadows across the worn carpet, the darkness pressing in around her, the air cold, suffocating, the silence sharp, brittle, the air heavy with secrets.

Mrs. Whitmore shuffled into the room, her thin, bony frame wrapped in a faded floral shawl, her sharp, piercing eyes fixed on Grace, her jaw clenched, her breath coming in short, shallow gasps, her pulse racing, her heart pounding, her mind spinning, the darkness pressing in around her, her world crumbling beneath her feet.

"Sit," the old woman said, her voice low, sharp, tense, a cold, hard edge to her words, her eyes dark, hard, her jaw clenched, her bony fingers curling tightly around the edge of her shawl, her breath coming in short, shallow gasps, her pulse racing, her heart pounding, her mind spinning, the darkness pressing in around her, her world crumbling beneath her feet.

Grace hesitated for a moment, her pulse quickening, her heart pounding, her breath catching in her throat, her mind spinning, the air around her growing thick, suffocating, the darkness pressing in around her, her world crumbling beneath her feet.

She sat.

Mrs. Whitmore lowered herself into a creaky, threadbare armchair, her thin, bony fingers gripping the arms of the chair, her jaw clenched, her eyes dark, hard, her breath coming in short, shallow gasps, her pulse racing, her heart pounding, her mind spinning, the darkness pressing in around her, her world crumbling beneath her feet.

The old woman's eyes narrowed, her thin, wrinkled lips curling into a tight, twisted smile, her breath coming in short, shallow gasps, her pulse racing, her heart pounding, her mind spinning, the darkness pressing in around her, her world crumbling beneath her feet.

"You're here about David," Mrs. Whitmore said, her voice low, sharp, tense, a cold, hard edge to her words, her jaw clenched, her eyes dark, hard, her breath coming in short, shallow gasps, her pulse racing, her heart pounding, her mind spinning, the darkness pressing in around her, her world crumbling beneath her feet.

Grace's heart skipped a beat, her pulse racing, her breath catching in her throat, her mind spinning, the air around her growing thick, suffocating, the darkness pressing in around her, her world crumbling beneath her feet.

"Yes," Grace said, her voice trembling, her words shaky, her breath catching in her throat, her pulse racing, her heart pounding, her mind spinning, the air around her growing thick, suffocating, the darkness pressing in around her, her world crumbling beneath her feet.

Mrs. Whitmore's thin, bony fingers tightened around the arms of her chair, her jaw clenched, her eyes dark, hard, her breath coming in short, shallow gasps, her pulse racing, her heart pounding, her mind spinning, the darkness pressing in around her, her world crumbling beneath her feet.

"You think you know him," the old woman said, her voice low, sharp, tense, a cold, hard edge to her words, her jaw clenched, her eyes dark, hard, her breath coming in short, shallow gasps, her pulse racing, her heart pounding, her mind spinning, the darkness pressing in around her, her world crumbling beneath her feet.

Grace's breath caught in her throat, her pulse racing, her heart pounding, her mind spinning, the air around her growing thick, suffocating, the darkness pressing in around her, her world crumbling beneath her feet.

"You have no idea," Mrs. Whitmore whispered, her voice trembling, her words shaky, her breath catching in her throat, her pulse racing, her heart pounding, her mind spinning, the air around her growing thick, suffocating, the darkness pressing in around her, her world crumbling beneath her feet.

Grace's jaw clenched, her fingers curling into tight, white-knuckled fists, her pulse racing, her heart pounding, her breath coming in short, shallow gasps, her mind spinning, the air around her growing thick, suffocating, the darkness pressing in around her, her world crumbling beneath her feet.

"Tell me," Grace said, her voice trembling, her words shaky, her breath catching in her throat, her pulse racing, her heart pounding, her mind spinning, the air around her growing thick, suffocating, the darkness pressing in around her, her world crumbling beneath her feet.

Mrs. Whitmore leaned forward, her thin, bony fingers tightening around the arms of her chair, her jaw clenched, her eyes dark, hard, her breath coming in short, shallow gasps, her pulse racing, her heart pounding, her mind spinning, the darkness pressing in around her, her world crumbling beneath her feet.

"He came to me once, years ago," the old woman whispered, her voice trembling, her words shaky, her breath catching in her throat, her pulse racing, her heart pounding, her mind spinning, the air around her growing thick, suffocating, the darkness pressing in around her, her world crumbling beneath her feet.

Grace's heart skipped a beat, her pulse racing, her breath catching in her throat, her mind spinning, the air around her growing thick, suffocating, the darkness pressing in around her, her world crumbling beneath her feet.

"What do you mean?" Grace whispered, her voice trembling, her words shaky, her breath catching in her throat, her pulse racing, her heart pounding, her mind spinning, the air around her growing thick, suffocating, the darkness pressing in around her, her world crumbling beneath her feet.

Mrs. Whitmore's thin, bony fingers tightened around the arms of her chair, her jaw clenched, her eyes dark, hard, her breath coming in short, shallow gasps, her pulse racing, her heart pounding, her mind spinning, the darkness pressing in around her, her world crumbling beneath her feet.

"He came to me for help," the old woman whispered, her voice trembling, her words shaky, her breath catching in her throat, her pulse racing, her heart pounding, her mind spinning, the air around her growing thick, suffocating, the darkness pressing in around her, her world crumbling beneath her feet.

Grace's jaw clenched, her fingers curling into tight, white-knuckled fists, her pulse racing, her heart pounding, her breath coming in short, shallow gasps, her mind spinning, the air around her growing thick, suffocating, the darkness pressing in around her, her world crumbling beneath her feet.

"What kind of help?" Grace whispered, her voice trembling, her words shaky, her breath catching in her throat, her pulse racing, her heart pounding, her mind spinning, the air around her growing thick, suffocating, the darkness pressing in around her, her world crumbling beneath her feet.

Mrs. Whitmore's thin, bony fingers tightened around the arms of her chair, her jaw clenched, her eyes dark, hard, her breath coming in short, shallow gasps, her pulse racing, her heart pounding, her mind spinning, the air around her growing thick, suffocating, the darkness pressing in around her, her world crumbling beneath her feet.

"To make something... disappear," the old woman whispered, her voice trembling, her words shaky, her breath catching in her throat, her pulse racing, her heart pounding, her mind spinning, the air around her growing thick, suffocating, the darkness pressing in around her, her world crumbling beneath her feet.

The air in Mrs. Whitmore's living room grew heavier, the dim light casting long, twisted shadows against the cracked wallpaper. Grace's pulse raced, her breath coming in short, shallow gasps, her mind spinning, the room closing in around her, the darkness pressing against her, the weight of Mrs. Whitmore's words settling heavily on her shoulders.

"To make something... disappear," the old woman whispered again, her voice trembling, her bony fingers gripping the arms of her chair so tightly that her knuckles turned white, the veins on the back of her hands standing out like twisted roots, her eyes dark, hollow, the air around her growing thick, suffocating, the darkness pressing in around her, her world crumbling beneath her feet.

Grace leaned forward, her jaw clenched, her breath coming in sharp, ragged gasps, her pulse pounding in her ears, the air around her thick, suffocating, the darkness pressing in around her, her world crumbling beneath her feet.

"What did he want you to hide?" Grace whispered, her voice trembling, her words shaky, her breath catching in her throat, her pulse racing, her heart pounding, her mind spinning, the air around her growing thick, suffocating, the darkness pressing in around her, her world crumbling beneath her feet.

Mrs. Whitmore's eyes narrowed, her thin, wrinkled lips curling into a tight, twisted smile, her breath coming in short, shallow gasps, her pulse racing, her heart pounding, her mind spinning, the darkness pressing in around her, her world crumbling beneath her feet.

"Not what, my dear," the old woman whispered, her voice trembling, her words shaky, her breath catching in her throat, her pulse racing, her heart pounding, her mind spinning, the air around her growing thick, suffocating, the darkness pressing in around her, her world crumbling beneath her feet. "Who."

Grace's heart skipped a beat, her pulse racing, her breath catching in her throat, her mind spinning, the air around her growing thick, suffocating, the darkness pressing in around her, her world crumbling beneath her feet.

"Who?" Grace whispered, her voice trembling, her words shaky, her breath catching in her throat, her pulse racing, her heart pounding, her mind spinning, the air around her growing thick, suffocating, the darkness pressing in around her, her world crumbling beneath her feet.

Mrs. Whitmore leaned back in her chair, her thin, bony fingers relaxing, her jaw unclenching, her eyes softening, her breath coming in long, slow, steady gasps, her pulse slowing, her heart calming, her mind clearing, the darkness retreating, her world steadying beneath her feet.

"It was years ago," the old woman said, her voice low, her words steady, her breath coming in long, slow, even gasps, her pulse calm, her heart steady, her mind clear, the darkness retreating, her world steadying beneath her feet. "David came to me, desperate, terrified, a man on the edge, his mind unraveling, his world crumbling around him."

Grace's jaw clenched, her breath catching in her throat, her pulse racing, her heart pounding, her mind spinning, the air around her growing thick, suffocating, the darkness pressing in around her, her world crumbling beneath her feet.

"He had done something," Mrs. Whitmore whispered, her voice trembling, her words shaky, her breath catching in her throat, her pulse racing, her heart pounding, her mind spinning, the air around her growing thick, suffocating, the darkness pressing in around her, her world crumbling beneath her feet. "Something terrible."

Grace's pulse raced, her breath coming in short, shallow gasps, her mind spinning, the air around her thick, suffocating, the darkness pressing in around her, her world crumbling beneath her feet.

"What did he do?" Grace whispered, her voice trembling, her words shaky, her breath catching in her throat, her pulse racing, her heart pounding, her mind spinning, the air around her growing thick, suffocating, the darkness pressing in around her, her world crumbling beneath her feet.

Mrs. Whitmore leaned forward, her thin, bony fingers tightening around the arms of her chair, her jaw clenched, her eyes dark, hard, her breath coming in short, shallow gasps, her pulse racing, her heart pounding, her mind spinning, the darkness pressing in around her, her world crumbling beneath her feet.

"He made someone... disappear," the old woman whispered, her voice trembling, her words shaky, her breath catching in her throat, her pulse racing, her heart pounding, her mind spinning, the air around her growing thick, suffocating, the darkness pressing in around her, her world crumbling beneath her feet.

Grace's heart skipped a beat, her pulse racing, her breath

catching in her throat, her mind spinning, the air around her thick, suffocating, the darkness pressing in around her, her world crumbling beneath her feet.

"Who?" Grace whispered, her voice trembling, her words shaky, her breath catching in her throat, her pulse racing, her heart pounding, her mind spinning, the air around her thick, suffocating, the darkness pressing in around her, her world crumbling beneath her feet.

Mrs. Whitmore's eyes narrowed, her thin, wrinkled lips curling into a tight, twisted smile, her breath coming in short, shallow gasps, her pulse racing, her heart pounding, her mind spinning, the darkness pressing in around her, her world crumbling beneath her feet.

"His first wife," the old woman whispered, her voice trembling, her words shaky, her breath catching in her throat, her pulse racing, her heart pounding, her mind spinning, the air around her thick, suffocating, the darkness pressing in around her, her world crumbling beneath her feet.

Grace's jaw dropped, her heart stopping, her pulse freezing, her breath catching in her throat, her mind spinning, the air around her thick, suffocating, the darkness pressing in around her, her world crumbling beneath her feet.

"He never told you about her, did he?" Mrs. Whitmore whispered, her voice trembling, her words shaky, her breath catching in her throat, her pulse racing, her heart pounding, her mind spinning, the air around her thick, suffocating, the darkness pressing in around her, her world crumbling beneath her feet.

CHAPTER 26

Shadows of the Past

The heavy door of the attic creaked open, dust particles swirling in the thin shaft of light from the single grimy window. Grace hesitated at the threshold, the air thick with the musty scent of forgotten years, the old wooden beams above her head groaning softly, the house itself whispering its secrets. She flicked on the flashlight she had hastily grabbed from the kitchen drawer, the harsh white beam cutting through the darkness, revealing cobweb-draped corners and stacks of dusty boxes piled high against the walls.

She had never been up here before. David had always dismissed the attic as a cluttered, forgotten space filled with old junk from the previous owners, a place best left alone. But now, with Mrs. Whitmore's words echoing in her mind – *"He made someone... disappear... his first wife."* – Grace felt compelled to dig deeper, to uncover the truth behind her husband's carefully constructed facade.

She stepped cautiously into the darkness, the wooden floorboards creaking beneath her feet, the air growing colder, the shadows closing in around her. She aimed the flashlight at the stacks of boxes, each one coated in a thick layer of dust, their sides yellowed with age, their corners frayed and bent, the faint outlines of forgotten memories etched into their surfaces.

She pulled down the first box, the cardboard sides sagging under the weight of its contents, the top flaps curling slightly, the tape brittle and peeling. She peeled back the lid, her heart pounding, her breath coming in short, shallow gasps, the darkness pressing in around her, her world crumbling beneath her feet.

Inside, she found a collection of old photo albums, the covers cracked and faded, their spines splitting, the pages yellowed with age, the corners curled, the edges frayed. She flipped open the first album, the plastic sleeves sticking together, the photos within dull and faded, the images blurred, the colors washed out.

At first, the pictures seemed innocent enough – a much younger David, his hair darker, his face unlined, his smile bright and carefree, his arm wrapped around a beautiful woman with long, dark hair and striking green eyes, her smile radiant, her laughter frozen in time, her eyes bright and alive, her world full of promise.

But as Grace turned the pages, her pulse quickened, her breath catching in her throat, her heart pounding, her mind spinning, the darkness pressing in around her, her world crumbling beneath her feet. She recognized the woman in the photographs – the same face, the same eyes, the same smile she had seen in the framed photos on Mrs. Whitmore's mantelpiece, the woman the old neighbor had called *Amelia.*

The name hit Grace like a punch to the gut, her knees trembling, her hands shaking, her breath coming in sharp, ragged gasps, the air around her growing thick, suffocating, the darkness pressing in around her, her world crumbling beneath her feet.

She flipped quickly through the rest of the album, the photos becoming darker, more haunting, the woman's bright smile fading, her eyes growing hollow, her face gaunt, her body thin, her spirit broken, the light in her eyes dimming, the darkness consuming her, her world crumbling around her.

One photo in particular stopped Grace cold – a black-and-white image, the edges frayed, the corners curled, the ink fading, the shadows deep, the scene haunting. It showed David and Amelia standing together in front of a large, crumbling house, their faces shadowed, their eyes hollow, their bodies stiff, their smiles forced, the darkness closing in around them, their world crumbling beneath their feet.

Grace's hands shook, her breath coming in short, shallow gasps, her pulse racing, her heart pounding, her mind spinning, the air around her growing thick, suffocating, the darkness pressing in around her, her world crumbling beneath her feet.

She flipped the photo over, her pulse racing, her breath catching in her throat, her heart pounding, her mind spinning, the air around her thick, suffocating, the darkness pressing in around her, her world crumbling beneath her feet.

Scrawled on the back, in a tight, hurried hand, were the words: *"Together forever, until the end."*

Grace's heart stopped, her pulse freezing, her breath catching in her throat, her mind spinning, the air around her thick, suffocating, the darkness pressing in around her, her world crumbling beneath her feet.

She dropped the album, the pages fluttering, the photos scattering, the darkness closing in around her, her world crumbling beneath her feet. She stumbled back, her breath coming in short, shallow gasps, her pulse racing, her heart pounding, her mind spinning, the air around her thick, suffocating, the darkness pressing in around her, her world crumbling beneath her feet.

The attic door creaked, the hinges groaning, the darkness pressing in around her, her world crumbling beneath her feet. She turned, her pulse racing, her breath catching in her throat, her heart pounding, her mind spinning, the air around her thick, suffocating, the darkness pressing in around her, her world crumbling beneath her feet.

And there, in the doorway, his silhouette framed by the thin shaft of light from the single grimy window, his eyes dark, his jaw clenched, his fists tight, his breath coming in short, shallow gasps, his pulse racing, his heart pounding, his mind spinning, the darkness pressing in around him, his world crumbling beneath his feet – stood David.

Grace clutched the edge of the kitchen counter, her fingers digging into the cool granite, her pulse pounding in her ears, her mind racing with a thousand fractured thoughts. The house was too quiet, the walls closing in around her, the shadows stretching long and sharp, the air thick with the weight of unspoken truths.

David had disappeared into the night, his silhouette swallowed by the darkness beyond their porch, his footsteps echoing down the gravel path, his breath coming in short, shallow gasps, his pulse racing, his heart pounding, his mind spinning, the air around him thick, suffocating, the darkness pressing in around him, his world crumbling beneath his feet.

She turned, her breath coming in sharp, ragged gasps, her pulse racing, her heart pounding, her mind spinning, the air around her thick, suffocating, the darkness pressing in around her, her world crumbling beneath her feet. Her eyes fell on the pile of scattered photographs on the kitchen table, the images burned into her mind, the faces haunting her, the shadows whispering her name, her world crumbling beneath her feet.

She grabbed her phone, her hands shaking, her breath catching in her throat, her pulse racing, her heart pounding, her mind spinning, the air around her thick, suffocating, the darkness pressing in around her, her world crumbling beneath her feet. She dialed Mrs. Whitmore's number, the old woman's words echoing in her mind, her voice sharp and clear, her tone cutting, her eyes hollow, her soul broken, her world crumbling beneath her feet.

The phone rang, the sound sharp and shrill, the line crackling, the darkness pressing in around her, her world crumbling beneath her feet. She held her breath, her pulse racing, her heart pounding, her mind spinning, the air around her thick, suffocating, the darkness pressing in around her, her world crumbling beneath her feet.

Finally, a weak, trembling voice crackled through the line, the words slow and uncertain, the tone shaky and frail, the darkness pressing in around her, her world crumbling beneath her feet.

"Hello?" Mrs. Whitmore's voice was thin, the sound weak and uncertain, the air around her thick, suffocating, the darkness pressing in around her, her world crumbling beneath her feet.

"Mrs. Whitmore," Grace whispered, her breath coming in short, shallow gasps, her pulse racing, her heart pounding, her mind spinning, the air around her thick, suffocating, the darkness pressing in around her, her world crumbling beneath her feet. "You were right... about everything."

A long, sharp intake of breath crackled through the line, the sound sharp and piercing, the air around her thick, suffocating, the darkness pressing in around her, her world crumbling beneath her feet.

"I tried to warn you, dear," Mrs. Whitmore's voice trembled, the words sharp and cutting, the tone filled with years of regret, the darkness pressing in around her, her world crumbling beneath her feet. "He... he won't stop. He never stops."

Grace's pulse quickened, her breath catching in her throat, her heart pounding, her mind spinning, the air around her thick, suffocating, the darkness pressing in around her, her world crumbling beneath her feet.

"What do you mean?" she whispered, her voice shaking, her hands trembling, her breath coming in short, shallow gasps, her pulse racing, her heart pounding, her mind spinning, the air around her thick, suffocating, the darkness pressing in around her, her world crumbling beneath her feet.

"He... he did this before," Mrs. Whitmore's voice cracked, the words sharp and cutting, the tone filled with years of regret, the darkness pressing in around her, her world crumbling beneath her feet. "With Amelia. He... he took her life... piece by piece... until there was nothing left."

The line crackled, the sound sharp and piercing, the air around her thick, suffocating, the darkness pressing in around her, her world crumbling beneath her feet.

"But... but I can stop him," Grace whispered, her breath coming in sharp, ragged gasps, her pulse racing, her heart pounding, her mind spinning, the air around her thick, suffocating, the darkness pressing in around her, her world crumbling beneath her feet. "I can break the cycle."

Silence filled the line, the darkness pressing in around her, her world crumbling beneath her feet.

"Be careful, Grace," Mrs. Whitmore's voice trembled, the words sharp and cutting, the tone filled with years of regret, the darkness pressing in around her, her world crumbling beneath her feet. "He's... he's smarter than you think. And if he finds out... if he knows you're onto him... he won't stop."

The line went dead, the sound sharp and piercing, the air around her thick, suffocating, the darkness pressing in around her, her world crumbling beneath her feet.

Grace dropped the phone, her breath coming in short, shallow gasps, her pulse racing, her heart pounding, her mind spinning, the air around her thick, suffocating, the darkness pressing in around her, her world crumbling beneath her feet.

She turned, her eyes falling on the front door, the darkness pressing in around her, her world crumbling beneath her feet. She took a step forward, her breath coming in sharp, ragged gasps, her pulse racing, her heart pounding, her mind spinning, the air around her thick, suffocating, the darkness pressing in around her, her world crumbling beneath her feet.

She would confront David. She would demand the truth. She would break the cycle.

And if he tried to stop her... she would make him pay.

To be continued in the next Series........coming soon

AUTHOR'S NOTE

Some secrets are spoken with silence. Others are hidden in plain sight—behind a gaze, a touch, or a lie we tell ourselves to survive.

The Eyes That Kept a Secret was born out of my fascination with the **power of perception**—how what we see, or choose not to see, shapes the truth we live. I've always been intrigued by the delicate line between **what is real and what we convince ourselves is real**, especially in intimate relationships. This story explores that line.

Through David and Grace's journey, I wanted to dive into the complexities of love, betrayal, vulnerability, and the masks we wear to protect the versions of ourselves we want others to see. What happens when the illusion breaks? When sight returns—literally or metaphorically—can we handle the truth it reveals?

This novel isn't just about secrets. It's about **identity, transformation**, and the unsettling beauty of **awakening**—even when that awakening shatters everything we thought we knew.

To anyone who has ever questioned the truth behind a smile, or sensed a storm beneath still waters, this book is for you.

Thank you for choosing to step into the shadows and light with me. Let the eyes tell their truth.

— **Judge Manyonga** *Author of The Eyes That Kept a Secret*

ACKNOWLEDGEMENTS

Writing *The Eyes That Kept a Secret* has been an unforgettable journey of imagination, emotion, and perseverance. Though only one name graces the cover, many hearts and hands have shaped this book.

First and foremost, I give thanks to **God**, the author of all creativity and the One who gives vision even in the darkest places. Without divine inspiration, this story would have never found its breath.

To my family — thank you for your patience, support, and quiet understanding during the long hours I disappeared into the world of Windmere Lane. Your belief in me, even when I doubted myself, kept the pen moving.

To my close friends and early readers who offered feedback with love and honesty — you helped this book become sharper, deeper, and more human. Special thanks to those who asked the hard questions and challenged me to dig beneath the surface of every character's motive.

To **the readers** — you are the reason this story exists beyond my own thoughts. Whether you saw yourself in David, Grace, or Mrs. Whitmore, or whether you simply came along for the suspenseful ride, I'm truly grateful you chose to turn these pages. Thank you for trusting me with your time and curiosity.

To the countless unknown people — the quiet observers, the wounded healers, and those who carry secrets behind their eyes — this story was written with you in mind.

And lastly, to every writer still chasing a dream: keep writing, keep risking, and keep telling the stories only you can tell. The world is waiting.

With deep gratitude, **Judge Manyonga**